PORGY

DU BOSE HEYWARD

PORGY

DU BOSE HEYWARD

Decorated by
THEODORE NADEJEN

GROSSET & DUNLAP, *Publishers*
by arrangement with GEORGE H. DORAN COMPANY

Copyright, 1925
By George H. Doran Company

PORGY

PRINTED IN THE UNITED STATES OF AMERICA

FOR

DOROTHY HEYWARD

Porgy, Maria, and Bess,
Robbins, and Peter, and Crown;
Life was a three-stringed harp
Brought from the woods to town.

Marvelous tunes you rang
From passion, and death, and birth,
You who had laughed and wept
On the warm, brown lap of the earth.

Now in your untried hands
An instrument, terrible, new,
Is thrust by a master who frowns,
Demanding strange songs of you.

God of the White and Black,
Grant us great hearts on the way
That we may understand
Until you have learned to play.

I

PART I

PORGY lived in the Golden Age. Not the Golden Age of a remote and legendary past; nor yet the chimerical era treasured by every man past middle life, that never existed except in the heart of youth; but an age when men, not yet old, were boys in an ancient, beautiful city that time had forgotten before it destroyed.

In this city there persisted the Golden Age of many things, and not the least among them was that of beggary. In those days the profession was one with a tradition. A man begged, presumably, because he was hungry, much as a man of more energetic temperament became a stevedore from the same cause. His plea for help produced the simple reactions of a generous impulse, a movement of the hand, and the gift of a coin, instead of the elaborate and terrifying processes of organized philanthropy. His antecedents and his mental age were his own affair, and, in the majority of cases, he was as happily oblivious of one as of the other.

Had it all been otherwise, had Porgy come a generation, or even a score of years, later, there would have been a repetition of the old tragedy of genius without opportunity. For, as the artist is born with the vision of beauty, and the tradesman with an eye for barter, so was Porgy equipped by a beneficent providence for a career of mendicancy. Instead of the sturdy legs that would have predestined him for the life of a stevedore on one of the great cotton wharves, he had, when he entered the world, totally inadequate nether extremities, quick to catch the eye, and touch the ready sympathy of the passer-by. Either by birth, or through the application of a philosophy of life, he had acquired a personality that could not be ignored, one which at the same time interested and subtly disturbed. There was that about him which differentiated him from the hordes of fellow practitioners who competed with him for the notice of the tender-hearted. Where others bid eagerly for attention, and burst into voluble thanks and blessings, Porgy sat silent, rapt. There was something

Eastern and mystic about the intense introspection of his look. He never smiled, and he acknowledged gifts only by a slow lifting of the eyes that had odd shadows in them. He was black with the almost purple blackness of unadulterated Congo blood. His hands were very large and muscular, and, even when flexed idly in his lap, seemed shockingly formidable in contrast with his frail body. Unless one were unusually preoccupied at the moment of dropping a coin in his cup, he carried away in return a very definite, yet somewhat disquieting, impression: a sense of infinite patience, and beneath it the vibration of unrealized, but terrific, energy.

No one knew Porgy's age. No one remembered when he first made his appearance among the ranks of the local beggars. A woman who had married twenty years before remembered him because he had been seated on the church steps, and had given her a turn when she went in.

Once a child saw Porgy, and said suddenly, "What is he waiting for?" That expressed him better than anything else. He was waiting, waiting with the concentrating intensity of a burning-glass.

As consistent in the practice of his profession as any of the business and professional

men who were his most valued customers,
Porgy was to be found any morning, by the
first arrival in the financial district, against
the wall of the old apothecary shop that
stands at the corner of King Charles Street
and The Meeting House Road. Long custom, reinforced by an eye for the beautiful,
had endeared that spot to him. He would
sit there in the cool of the early hours and
look across the narrow thoroughfare into the
green freshness of Jasper Square, where the
children flew their kites, and played hide-
and-seek among the shrubs. Then, when the
morning advanced, and the sun poured its
semi-tropical heat between the twin rows of
brick, to lie impounded there, like a stagnant pool of flame, he would experience a
pleasant atavistic calm, and would doze
lightly under the terrific heat, as only a full-
blooded negro can. Toward afternoon a
slender blue shadow would commence to
grow about him that would broaden with
great rapidity, cool the baking flags, and turn
the tide of customers home before his empty
cup.

But Porgy best loved the late afternoons,
when the street was quiet again, and the
sunlight, deep with color, shot level over the
low roof of the apothecary shop to paint the
cream stucco on the opposite dwelling a

ruddy gold and turn the old rain-washed tiles on the roof to burnished copper. Then the slender, white-clad lady who lived in the house would throw open the deep French windows of the second story drawing-room, and sitting at the piano, where Porgy could see her dimly, she would play on through the dusk until old Peter drove by with his wagon to carry him home.

§

Porgy had but one vice. With his day reduced to the dead level of the commonplace, he was by night an inveterate gambler. Each evening his collections were carefully divided into a minimum for room and food, and the remainder for the evening's game. Seen in the light of the smoking kerosene lamp, with the circle of excited faces about him, he was no longer the beggar in the dust. His stagnant blood leaped to sudden life. He was the peer of the great, hulking fellows who swung cotton bales and stank intolerably from labor in the fertilizer mills. He even knew that he had won their grudging respect, for he had a way of coaxing and wheedling the little ivory cubes that forced them to respond. The loud "Oh, my Baby," and explosive "Come seben," of his fellowgamesters seldom brought silver when he experienced that light, keen feeling and thought of the new, soft-spoken words to say. In those hours he lost his look of living in the future. While the ivories flew, he existed in an intense and burning present.

One Saturday night in late April, with the first premonitory breath of summer in the air, Porgy sat in the gaming circle that had gathered before his door in Catfish Row, and murmured softly to his gods of chance. All day he had been conscious of a vague unrest. There had been no breeze from the bay, and from his seat outside the apothecary shop the sky showed opaque blue-grey and bore heavily upon the town. Towards evening, a thunder-head had lifted over the western horizon and growled ominously; but it had passed, leaving the air hot, vitiated, and moist. The negroes had come in for the night feeling irritable, and, instead of the usual Saturday night of song and talk, the rooms were for the most part dark and silent, and the court deserted.

The game started late, and there were few players. Opposite Porgy, sitting upon his haunches, and casting his dice in moody silence, was a negro called Crown. He was a stevedore, had the body of a gladiator, and a bad name. His cotton-hook, hanging from his belt by a thong, gleamed in the lamp-light, and rang a clear note on the flags when he leant forward to throw. Crown had been drinking with Robbins, who sat next to him, and the air was rank with the effluvium of vile corn whisky. Robbins was voluble, and as usual, when in liquor, talked incessantly of his wife and children, of whom he was inordinately proud. He was a good provider, and, except for his Saturday night drink and game, of steady habits.

"Dat lady ob mine is a born white-folks nigger," he boasted. "She fambly belong tuh Gob'ner Rutledge. Ain't yer see Miss Rutledge sheself come tuh visit she when she sick? An' dem chillen ob mine, dem is raise wid *ways*."

"Yo' bes sabe yo' talk for dem damn dice. Dice ain't gots no patience wid 'oman!" cut in a young negro of the group.

"Da's de trut'," called another. "Dey is all two after de same nigger money. Dat mek um can't git 'long."

"Shet yo' damn mout' an' t'row!" growled Crown.

Robbins, taken aback, rolled the dice hastily. Scarcely had they settled before Crown scooped them fiercely into his great hand, and, swearing foully at them, sent them tumbling out across the faintly illuminated circle, to lose them on the first cast. Then Porgy took them up tenderly, and held them for a moment cupped in his muscular, slim-fingered hand.

"Oh, little stars, roll me some light!" he sang softly; made a pass, and won. "Roll me a sun an' moon!" he urged; and again the cubes did his bidding.

"Porgy witch dem dice," Crown snarled, as he drained his flask and sent it shattering against the pavement.

Under the beetling walls of the tenement the game went swiftly forward. In a remote room several voices were singing drowsily, as though burdened by the oppression of the day. In another part of the building some one was picking a guitar monotonously, chord after chord, until the dark throbbed like an old wound. But the players were oblivious of all except the splash of orange light that fell upon the flags, and the living little cubes that flashed or dawdled upon it, according to the mood of the hand that propelled them. Peter, the old wagoner, sat quietly smoking in Porgy's doorway, and looked on with the indulgent smile of tolerant age. Once when Crown lost heavily, and turned snarling upon Robbins with, "T'row dem damn dice fair, nigger," he cautioned mildly, "Frien' an' licker an' dice ain't meant tuh 'sociate. Yo' mens bes' go slow."

Then, in a flash, it happened.

Robbins rolled again, called the dice, and retrieved them before Crown's slow wits got the count, then swept the heap of coins into his pocket.

With a low snarl, straight from his crouching position, Crown hurled his tremendous weight forward, shattering the lamp, and bowling Robbins over against the wall. Then they were up and facing each other. The oil from the broken lamp settled between two flags and blazed up ruddily. Crown was crouched for a second spring, with lips drawn from gleaming teeth. The light fell strong upon thrusting jaw, and threw the sloping brow into shadow. One hand touched the ground lightly, balancing the massive torso. The other arm held the cotton-hook forward, ready, like a prehensile claw. In comparison Robbins was pitifully slender and inadequate. There was a single desperate moment of indecision; then he took his only chance. Like a thrown spear, he hurled his lithe body forward under the terrifying hook, and clinched. Down, down, down the centuries they slid. Clothes could not hold them. Miraculously the tawny, ridged bodies tore through the thin coverings. Bronze ropes and bars slid and wove over great shoulders. Bright, ruddy planes leaped out on backs in the fire flare, then were gulped by sliding shadows. A heady, bestial stench absorbed all other odors. A fringe of shadowy watchers crept from cavernous doorways, sensed it, and commenced to wail eerily. Backward and forward, in a space no larger than a small room, the heaving, inseparable mass rocked and swayed. Breath labored like steam. At times the fused single body would thrust out a rigid arm, or the light would point out, for one hideous second, a tortured, mad face. Again the mass would rise as though propelled a short distance from the earth, topple, and crash down upon the pavement with a jarring impact.

Such terrific expenditure of human energy could not last. The end came quickly, and with startling suddenness. Crown broke his adversary's weakening hold, and held him the length of one mighty arm. The other swung the cotton-hook downward. Then he dropped his victim, and swaggered drunkenly toward the street. Even to the most inexperienced the result would have been obvious. Robbins was dead: horribly dead.

A scream rose to a crescendo of unendurable agony, and a woman broke through the circle of spectators and cast herself upon the body. The fire flickered to a faint, blue flame, unearthly, terrifying.

Porgy shivered violently, whimpered in the gloom; then drew himself across his threshold and closed the door.

§

Catfish Row, in which Porgy lived, was not a row at all, but a great brick structure that lifted its three stories about the three sides of a court. The fourth side was partly closed by a high wall, surmounted by jagged edges of broken glass set firmly in old lime plaster, and pierced in its center by a wide entrance-way. Over the entrance there still remained a massive grill of Italian wrought iron, and a battered capital of marble surmounted each of the lofty gate-posts. The court itself was paved with large flag-stones, which even beneath the accumulated grime of a century, glimmered with faint and varying pastel shades in direct sunlight. The south wall, which was always in shadow, was lichened from pavement to rotting gutter; and opposite, the northern face, unbroken except by rows of small-paned windows, showed every color through its flaking stucco, and, in summer, a steady blaze of scarlet from rows of geraniums that bloomed in old vegetable tins upon every window-sill.

Within the high-ceilinged rooms, with their battered colonial mantels and broken decorations of Adam designs in plaster, governors had come and gone, and ambassadors of kings had schemed and danced. Now before the gaping entrance lay only a narrow, cobbled street, and beyond, a tumbled wharf used by negro fishermen. Only the bay remained unchanged. Beyond the litter of the wharf, it stretched to the horizon, taking its mood from the changing skies; always different—invariably the same.

Directly within the entrance of the Row, and having upon the street a single bleary window, wherein were displayed plates of fried fish, was the "cook-shop" which catered to the residents of the tenement.

Porgy's room was opposite the shop and enjoyed the great advantage of having a front window that commanded the street and harbor, and an inner door where he could sit and enter into the life of the court. To him, the front window signified adventure, the door—home.

§

It was Porgy's custom, when the day's work was done and he had exchanged a part

of his collections for his evening meal of
fish and bread, to sit at his front .window
and watch the world pass by. The great
cotton wharves lay up the river, beyond the
Row; and when the cotton season was on, he
loved to sit in the dusk and see the drays
go by. They would sweep into view with
a loud thunder of wheels on the cobbles; and
from his low seat they loomed huge and
mysterious in the gathering dark. Sometimes there would be twenty of them in a
row, with great swiftly-stepping mules,
crouched figures of drivers, and bales piled
toweringly above them. Always Porgy experienced a vague and not unpleasant fear
when the drays swung past. There was
power, vast, awe-inspiring; it could so easily
crush him were he in its path. But here,
safe within his window, he could watch it
with perfect safety. At times when the train
was unusually long, the sustained, rhythmic
thunder and the sweep of form after form
past his window produced an odd pleas-
urable detachment in his mind, and pictures
of strange things and places would brighten
and fade. But the night following the killing, the window was closed, and through the
open door behind him beat the rhythm of a
dirge from Robbins' room.

"What de matter, chillen?" came the

strophe. And the antistrophe swelled to the answer:

"Pain gots de body, an' I can't stan' still."

Porgy sat upon his floor counting the day's collection: one dollar and twenty cents. It had been a good day. Perhaps the sorrow that had brooded over his spirit had quickened the sympathy of the passers-by.

"What de matter, Sister?"

"Jedus gots our brudder, an' I can't stan' still."

Ever since Porgy had come home the air had swung to the rhythm of the chant. He divided his pile into equal portions, and commenced to pocket one. The burden swayed out again.

"Pain gots de body, an' I can't stan' still."

He hesitated a moment, poured all the coins together again, selected a twenty-five-cent piece which he put into his pocket, and, taking the remainder in his hand, went out and drew himself across the short distance to the room of mourning.

The body lay upon a bed in the corner of the room, sheeted to the eyes, and upon its breast rested a large blue saucer. Standing in a circle about the bed, or seated upon the floor, backs to the wall, were a score of negroes, some singing, and others swaying, patting the floor with their large feet. For not a single moment since the body had been laid out had the rhythm slackened. With each hour it gathered weight until it seemed to swing the massive structure.

Porgy had heard that Robbins had left no burial insurance, the customary Saturday night festivities having consumed the slender margin between daily wage and immediate need. Now, at sight of the saucer, he knew that rumor had not erred. It had been an old custom among penniless negroes to prepare the corpse thus, then to sing dirges until neighborhood sympathy provided the wherewithal for proper interment. Recent years had introduced the insurance agent and the "buryin' lodge," and the old custom had fallen into disuse. It had even become a grievous reproach to have a member of the family a "saucer-buried nigger."

At the .foot of the bed, bowed by the double weight of sorrow and disgrace, the widow sat swaying to the rhythm like a beach palm in the ebb and flow of a bleak sea wind.

The sight of her grief, the close room, the awful presence beneath the sheet, and the unceasing pulse of sound that beat against his ears, all contributed to stir a strange desire into being within Porgy. Suddenly he threw his head back and wailed long and quaveringly. In rushed a vast feeling of relief. He wailed again, emptied his handful of small coins into the saucer, and sank to the floor at the head of the bed. Presently he commenced to croon with the others, and a sense of exaltation flooded his being, compelling him from the despair of the dirge to a more triumphant measure.

"Oh, I gots a little brudder in de new grabe-yahd. What outshine de sun," he sang.

Without missing the beat, the chorus shifted: "An' I'll meet um in the primus lan'."

Then came a rude interruption. A short yellow negro bustled into the room. His voice was low, oily, and penetrating. He was dressed entirely in black, and had an air of great importance. The song fell away to scarcely more than a throbbing silence. The man crossed the room to where the widow sat huddled at the foot of the bed, and touched her on the shoulder. She raised a face like a burned out ember.

"How de saucer stan' now, my sister?" he whispered, at the same time casting an appraising glance toward the subject of his inquiry.

"Dere ain't but fifteen dollar," she replied in a flat, despairing voice.

"An' he gots tuh git buried termorrer," called an awed voice, "or de boahd ob healt' will take um, an' give um tuh de students."

The widow's scream shrilled wildly. She rose to her knees and clutched the man's hand between both of hers. "Oh, fuh Gawd's sake bury um in de grabe-yahd. I goin' tuh work Monday, and I swear tuh Gawd I goin' tuh pay yuh ebery cent."

For a second even the rhythm ceased, leav-ing an aching suspense in the air. Watchers waited tensely. Wide eyes, riveted on the man's face, pleaded silently. Presently his professional manner slipped from him. "All right, Sister," he said simply. "Wid de box, an' one ca'age it will cost me more dan twenty-five. But I'll see yuh t'rough. Yuh can all be ready at eight tumorruh. It's a long trip tuh de cemetery."

The woman relaxed silently across the foot of the bed, her head between her out-flung arms. Then from the narrow confines of the room, the song beat up and out tri-umphantly:

"Oh, I gots a little brudder in de new grabe-yahd. What outshine de sun!"

The rhythm swelled, and voices in the

court and upper rooms took it up, until the
deeply-rooted old walls seemed to rock and
surge with the sweep of it.

§

In the cool of the early morning, the procession took its departure for the cemetery
that lay beyond the city limits to the north.
First went the dilapidated hearse, with its
rigid wooden plumes, and faded black velvet
draperies that nodded and swayed inside the
plate glass panels. Then followed the solitary carriage, in which could be seen massed
black accentuated by several pairs of white
cotton gloves held to lowered eyes. Behind
the carriage came the mourners in a motley
procession of wagons and buggies that had
been borrowed for the occasion.

Porgy drove with Peter, and four women,
seated on straight chairs in the wagon behind them, completed their company. From
time to time a long-drawn wail would rise
from one of the conveyances, to be taken up
and passed back from wagon to wagon like
a dismal echo.

Moving from the negro district into the
wide thoroughfare of Meeting House Road,
with its high buildings and its white faces
that massed and scattered on the pavements,

the cortége appeared almost grotesque, with the odd fusion of comedy and tragedy so inextricably a part of negro life in its deep moments.

The fat German who kept the shop on the corner of King Charles Street and Summer Road, called his clerk from the depths of the building, and their stomachs shook with laughter. But the little, dark Russian Jew in the next shop, who dealt in abominably smelling clothing, gave them a reproving look, and disappeared indoors.

The cemetery lay several miles beyond the city limits. The lot was bare of trees, but among the graves many bright flowering weeds masked the ugliness of the troubled earth. To the eastward a wide marsh stretched away to a far, bright line of sea. Westward, ploughed fields swept out to a distant forest of yellow pine. From the sea to the far tree tops, the sky swung a dizzy arch of thin blue, high in the center of which several buzzards hung motionless, watching.

In the vast emptiness of the morning the little procession crawled out to the edge of the broken wooden fence that marked the enclosure, and stopped.

By the time the last wagon had arrived, the cheap pine casket was resting upon battens over the grave, and the preacher, robed in white, was preparing to commence the service.

The mourners gathered close about the grave.

"Death, ain't yuh gots no shame?" called a clear, high, soprano voice; and immediately the mortal embodiment of infinite sorrow broke and swayed about the grave in the funeral chant. Three times the line swung its curve of song, shrill, keen, agonizing; then it fell away to a heart-wrenching minor on the burden:

"Take dis man an' gone—gone.
Death, ain't yuh gots no shame?"

When the singing ceased, the burial service commenced, the preacher extemporizing fluently. Taking his rhythm from the hymn, he poured his words along its interminable reiteration until the cumulative effect rocked the entire company.

The final moment of the ritual arrived. The lid was removed from the casket, and the mourners were formed into line to pass and look upon the face of the dead. A very old, bent negress went first. She stooped, then suddenly, with a shriek of anguish, cast herself beside the coffin.

"Tell Peter tuh hold de do' open fuh me. I's comin' soon!" she cried.

"Yes, Gawd, goin' soon," responded a voice in the crowd. Others pressed about the grave, and the air was stabbed by scream on scream. Grief spent itself freely, terrifyingly.

Slowly the clashing sounds merged into the regular measure of a spiritual. Beautiful and poignant it rose, swelling out above the sounds of falling earth as the grave was filled:

> "What yuh goin' ter do when yuh
>   come out de wilderness,
> Come out de wilderness,
> Come out de wilderness;
> What yuh goin' ter do when yuh
>   come out de wilderness
> Leanin' on my Lord.

> "Leanin' on my Lord,
> Leanin' on my Lord,
> Leanin' on my Lord
> Who died on Calvary."

The music faded away in vague, uncertain minors. The mood of the crowd changed almost tangibly. There was an air of restless apprehension. Nervous glances

were directed toward the entrance. Peter,
always sagacious, unless taken unawares, had
conferred in advance with Porgy about this
moment. When he had helped him from
the wagon, he had stationed him just inside
the fence, where he could be lifted quickly
into the road.

"De las' man in de grabe-yahd goin' tuh
be de nex' one tuh git buried," he had re-
minded his friend.

Now, as the final shovelful of earth was
thrown upon the grave, he came running to
Porgy, and lifted him quickly into the road.
Behind them broke a sudden earth-shaking
burst of sound, as of the stampeding of
many cattle, and past them the mourners
swept, stumbling, fighting for room; some
assisting weaker friends, others fighting savagely to be free of the enclosure. In the
center of the crowd, plunging forward with
robes flying, was the preacher. In an in-
credibly short time the lot was cleared.
Then, from a screening bush near the grave,
arose the old negress who had been the first
to wail out her grief. She had lain there
forgotten, overcome by the storm of her
emotion. She tottered feebly into the road.

"Nebber you min', Sister," the preacher
assured her comfortingly. "Gawd always
lub de righteous."

Dazed, and much pleased at the attention that she was receiving, while still happily unmindful of its cause, the old woman smiled a vague smile, and was hoisted into the wagon.

During the funeral the sun had disappeared behind clouds that had blown in swiftly from the sea, and now a scurry of large drops swept over the vehicles, and trailed away across the desolate graves.

"Dat's all right now fer Robbins," commented Porgy. "Gawd done sen' he rain already fuh wash he feet-steps offen dis eart'."

"Oh, yes, Brudder!" contributed a woman's voice; and, "Amen, my Jedus!" added another.

§

In the early afternoon of the day of the funeral, Porgy sat in his doorway communing with Peter. The old man was silent for awhile, his grizzled head bowed, and an expression of brooding tenderness upon his lined face.

"Robbins war a good man," he reflected at length, "an' dat nigger, Crown, war a killer, an' fuhebber gettin' intuh trouble. Yet, dere lie Robbins, wid he wife an'

fadderless chillen; an' Crown done gone he
ways tuh do de same t'ing ober again some-
wheres else."

"Gone fuh true. I reckon he done lose
now on Kittiwar Islan', in dem palmettuh
t'icket; an' de rope ain't nebber make fuh
ketch um an' hang um." Porgy stopped
suddenly, and motioned with his head
toward someone who had just entered the
court. The new arrival was a white man of
stocky build, wearing a wide-brimmed hat,
and a goatee. He was swinging a heavy
cane, and he crossed the court directly and
paused before the two. For a moment he
stood looking down at them with brows
drawn fiercely together. Then he drew back
his coat, exhibiting a police badge, and a
heavy revolver in a breast holster.

"You killed Robbins," he shot out suddenly at Peter. "And I'm going to hang
you for it. Come along now!" and he
reached out and laid a firm hand upon the
old man's shoulder.

Peter shook violently, and his eyes rolled
in his head. He made an ineffectual effort
to speak, tried again, and finally said,
" 'Fore Gawd, Boss, I ain't nebber done it."

Like a flash, the pistol was out of its
holster, and pointing between his eyes.
"Who did it, then?" snapped the man.

"Crown, Boss. I done see him do um," Peter cried in utter panic.

The man laughed shortly. "I thought so," he said. Then he turned to Porgy.

"You saw it too, eh?"

There was panic in Porgy's face, and in his lap his hands had clinched upon each other. But his eyes were fixed upon the paving. He drew a deep breath, and waited.

A flare of anger swept the face above him. "Come. Out with it. I don't want to have to put the law on you."

Porgy's only answer was a slight tremor that shook the hands in his lap. The detective's face darkened, and sweat showed under his hat-brim. Suddenly his temper bolted.

"Look at me, you damned nigger!" he shouted.

Slowly the sitting figure before him relaxed, almost it seemed, muscle by muscle. At last the hands fell apart, and lay flexed and idle. Finally Porgy raised eyes that had become hard and impenetrable as onyx. They met the angry glare that beat down upon them without flinching. After a long moment, he spoke slowly, and with great quietness.

"I ain't know nuttin' 'bout um. I been

inside, asleep on my bed, wid de do' closed."

"You're a damn liar," the man snapped.

He shrilled a whistle, and two policemen entered.

"He saw the killing," the detective said, indicating Peter. "Take him along, and lock him up as a material witness."

"How about the cripple?" asked one of the officers.

"He could not have helped seeing it," the man said sourly. "That's his room right there. But I can't make him come through. But it don't matter. One's enough to hang Crown, if we ever get him. Come, get the old man in the wagon."

The policeman lifted the shaking old negro to his feet. "Come along, Uncle. It ain't going to be as bad for you as Crown, anyway," encouraged one of them. Then the little party passed out of the entrance, leaving Porgy alone.

From the street sounded the shrill gong of the patrol wagon, followed by the beat of swiftly receding hoofs upon the cobbles.

§

Ten days had passed since the detective had taken Peter away. For a week the wagon had waited under the tottering shed, and the dejected old horse had subsisted upon a varied diet brought to him by the friends of his absent master. Then a man had come and taken the outfit away. In answer to the protests of the negroes, he had exhibited a contract, dated three years previous, by which Peter was to pay two dollars a week for an indefinite period, on an exorbitant purchase price. Failure to pay any installment would cause the property to revert to the seller. It all looked thoroughly legal. And so the dilapidated old rig rattled over the cobbles and departed.

Then the man from the installment furniture house came. He was a vile-mouthed, bearded Teuton, and swore so fiercely that no one dared to protest when he loaded Peter's furniture on his truck and drove away.

Now there remained in a corner of Porgy's room, where he had taken them into custody, only a battered leather trunk, a chromo of "The Great Emancipator," and a bundle of old clothes; mute reminders of their kindly and gentle old owner.

II

PART II

THE languor of a Southern May was in
the air. It was a season dear to the
heart of a negro. Work on the wharves was
slowing down, and the men were putting in
only two or three days a week. There were
always some of them lying about the court,
basking in the sun, laughing, and telling
stories while they waited for their women
to come from the "white folks'" kitchens,
with their full dinner pails.

Near the entrance, the stevedores usually
lounged, their great size differentiating them
from most of the other men. They had
bright bandanas about their thick necks, and
under their blue cotton shirts moved broad,
flat backs that could heft a five hundred
pound cotton bale. Earning more money
than the others, and possessing vast physical
strength in a world of brute force, they
lorded it swaggeringly about the court; taking the women that they wanted, and dress-
ing them gorgeously in the clashing crim-
sons and purples that they loved.

Grief over the loss of Robbins had
stormed itself out at the funeral. Peter's ill

fortune still occasioned general comment,
but slight concern to the individual. There
was an air of gaiety about. The scarlet of
the geraniums was commencing to flicker
in a run of windy flame on each window
sill; and from the bay came the smell of
salt air blown across young marsh-grass.

At the wharf, across the narrow street,
the fishermen were discharging strings of
gleaming whiting and porgy. Vegetable
sloops, blowing up from the Sea Islands,
with patched and tawny sails, broke the flat
cobalt of the inner harbor with the cross-
wash of their creamy wakes.

Through the back door of the cook-shop
Maria, the huge proprietress, could be seen
cutting shark-steaks from a four-foot ham-
mer-head that one of the fishermen had given
her. All in all, it was a season for the good
things of life, to be had now for scarcely
more than the asking.

Only Porgy sat lonely and disconsolate in
his doorway and watched the sunlight creep
up the eastern wall until it faded to a faint
red at the top, then the blue dusk grew under
the wharf, and swirled through the street
and court. He had not been able to get to
his stand since Peter's departure; and the
small store of coins, which he kept under a
loose brick in his hearth, was nearing ex-

haustion. Also, he missed his old friend
keenly and could not enter into the light-
hearted life about him.

Presently two women entered. Porgy
saw that they were Robbins' widow, and
her sister, who now shared her room. He
had been awaiting their coming eagerly, as
they had left in the early afternoon to carry
bed-clothing and food to the jail for Peter.

"How yuh fin' um, Sister?" he hailed.

The younger woman paused, standing in
the shadow, and the widow lowered herself
to a seat beside Porgy. She had put her
grief aside, and gone resolutely about her
task of earning a living for the three children.

"I can't puzzle dis t'ing out," she said
after a while. "De old man ain't done nuttin', an' dey done gots um lock up like a
chicken t'ief. Dey say dey gots tuh keep
um till dat nigger Crown get ketch; an,
Gawd knows when dat debble ob a t'ing
goin' tuh happen."

"It sho pay nigger tuh go blin' in dis
world," contributed the young woman.
"Porgy ain't gots much leg, but he sho got
sense."

After a moment of reflection, Porgy replied: "Sense do berry well; but he can't
lift no weight."

A big stevedore was crossing the court, his body moving easily with the panther-like flow of enormous muscular power under absolute control.

The beggar's eyes became wistful.

"Sense gots power tuh take a t'ing atter yuh gits dere," he said. "But he nebber puts bittle in a belly what can't leabe he restin' place. What I goin' do now sence Peter gone, an' I can't git on de street?"

"Pray, Brudder, pray," said the widow devoutly. "Ain't yuh see Gawd done soffen de haht of dat yalluh buryin' ondehtakuh attuh I done pray tuh him fuh a whole day an' night? Gawd gots leg fuh de cripple."

"Bless de Lord!" ejaculated the young woman.

"An' he gots comfort fuh de widder."

"Oh, my Jedus!" crooned Porgy, beginning to sway.

"An' food fuh de fadderless."

"Yes, Lord!"

"An' he goin' raise dis poor nigger out de dus'."

"Allelujah!"

"An' set um in de seat ob de righteous."

"Amen, my Sister!"

For a little while the three figures, showing now only as denser shadows in a world of shade, swayed slowly from side to side.

Then, without saying a word, Porgy drew himself across his threshold, and closed the door very softly.

§

It was not yet day when Porgy awakened suddenly. His eyes were wide, and his face was working with unwonted emotion. In the faint light that penetrated his bleared window from a street lamp, he made his way to the hearth, and removed the brick from his secret depository. With feverish haste he counted his little store, placing the coins in a row before him. Then with the utmost care he recounted them, placing them in little piles, one for the coppers, one for the nickels, and one for the dimes. When he had fully satisfied himself as to the extent of his wealth, his tension relaxed, and, tying the money in a rag which he tore from his bed-clothing, he closed his hand firmly upon it, crawled back into bed, and immediately fell asleep.

§

Two days later, Porgy drove his chariot out through the wide entrance into a land of romance and adventure. He was seated

with the utmost gravity in an inverted pack-
ing-case that proclaimed with unconscious
irony the virtues of a well-known toilet
soap. Beneath the box two solid lop-sided
wheels turned heavily. Before him, between a pair of improvised shafts, a patri-
archal goat tugged with the dogged per-
sistence of age which has been placed upon
its mettle, and flaunted an intolerable stench
in the face of the complaisant and virtuous
soap box.

As oblivious of the mirth-provoking quality of his appearance, as he was of a smell to
which custom had inured him, Porgy turned
his equipage daringly into a new thoroughfare, and drove through a street where high,
bright buildings stood between wide gardens,
and where many ladies passed and re-passed
on the sidewalks, or in glittering carriages.

But the magic that had come to pass, even
in the triumph of that first morning, stirred
vague doubts and misgivings within him.
He noticed that while he occasioned slight
comment in the negro quarter, no sooner had
he entered the white zone, than people commenced to pass him with averted faces, and
expressions that struggled between pity and
laughter. When he finally reached his old
stand before the apothecary shop, these misgivings crystallized into a definite fear.

Several of his clients happened to be passing the shop together. One of them was clerk to an apothecary further down the street. He seized his nose with one hand, while he pointed at Porgy with the other. Then all seized their noses, shaking with laughter, and waited to see what would happen.

Porgy looked his outfit over carefully. Certainly it was working with the utmost satisfaction. Somewhat mystified, he tied the ancient animal to a post, and, with great gravity, swung himself out of his wagon, across the pavement, and to his old stand.

The boys who had laughed stood nearby, and were joined by others, until soon there was quite a group.

Presently there issued from the shop the loud voice of the proprietor: "Oh, Mary, come quick, and bring the broom. Something has died again." Then followed the sound of boxes being overturned, while dust from a prodigious sweeping bellied in clouds from the door. Then the apothecary, very red in the face, came out for air, and found the goat. The burst of laughter that greeted him increased his irritation. Brandishing the broom, and in no uncertain language, he drove Porgy from his door.

But the bystanders had so enjoyed the

joke at the apothecary's expense, and were feeling in such high good humor, that when Porgy had an opportunity to appraise his collections, he found that they amounted to more than he frequently got from a whole day of patient waiting.

§

It is impossible to conceive of a more radical change than that brought about in Porgy's life by his new emancipation. From his old circumstances which had conspired to anchor him always to one spot, he was now in the grip of new forces that as inevitably resulted in constant change of scene. Soon he became quite a metropolitan, and might have been seen in any part of the city, either sitting in his wagon at the curb, or, if the residents of the locality seemed lenient in their attitude toward goats, disembarking, and trying his luck in the strip of shade along the wall.

In those days, everyone tolerated Porgy—for a while. He had become "a character." The other beggars gnashed their teeth, but were powerless.

On certain days he would turn to the south when he left the court, and soon would emerge into a land of such beauty that he never lost the illusion that it was unreal. No one seemed to work in that country, except the happy, well-clothed negroes who frequently came to back gates when he passed, and gave him tender morsels from the white folks' kitchens. The great, gleaming houses looked out at him with kindly eyes that peered between solid walls of climbing roses. Ladies on the deep piazzas would frequently send a servant running out to give him a coin and speed him on his way.

Before the houses and the rose-trellises stretched a broad drive, and beyond its dazzling belt of crushed shell the harbor lay between its tawny islands, like a sapphire upon a sailor's weathered hand. Sometimes Porgy would steal an hour from the daily rounds, pause there, and watch a great, blunt-nosed steamer heave slowly out of the unknown, to come to rest with a sigh of spent steam, and a dusty thundering of released anchor chains.

"Gawd sho gots a long arm," he would murmur; or, "Porgy, yo' sho is a little somethin' aftuh all."

Then there would be other days when he would repair to the narrow retail street, with its unbelievable windows, and drawing near to the curb, between the tall carriages of the shoppers would fall heir to the pennies which they got with their change, and which were of no value to such as they.

Always kind hands dropped coins in his cup, and sped him on. They were great days for Porgy. And great were the nights when he would tell of his adventures to the envious circle that gathered in the dusk of the court.

But Porgy was by nature a dreamer, and there were times even in those days, when his mind returned with wistful longing to the old uninterrupted hours when he used to sit, lost in meditation, under the unmarked drift of time. Some day, he would tell himself, there would come one with a compassion so great that he would give both Porgy and the goat place by his doorstep. Then life would be perfect indeed.

§

June, and the cotton season was over. The last tramp steamer had faded into the horizon. Great sheds that linked land and sea lay empty and dark, and through their cavernous depths echoed the thud and suck of waves against the bulkheads. The last of the stevedores had departed, some to the plantations, others to the phosphate mines, and still others to the river barges.

The long, hot days, so conducive to indolence, brought a new phase of life to Catfish Row. The loud talk and noisy comings and goings diminished. Men came in earlier in the evenings, and spent more time with their women.

Porgy sat alone in his doorway. In a room overhead a man and his wife were engaged in a friendly quarrel that ended in laughter. From an open window nearby came the sound of drowsy child voices. In the crowded dark about him, Life, with cruel preoccupation, was engrossed with its eternal business.

A large, matronly woman who lived near him, passed, carrying a pail of water. She stopped, set down her burden, and dropped a hand on Porgy's shoulder.

"What de matter wid dis man, he ain't gots nuttin' tuh say?" she asked him kindly.

Porgy's face contracted with emotion. He caught her hand and hurled it from him. "Lemme be," he rasped, in a tight, husky voice. "Yuh done gots yuh own man. Ain't yuh?"

"Oh, Lawd!" she laughed, as she turned away. "Yuh ain't t'ink I wantin' *yuh*, is yuh? Do listen tuh de man."

§

Through the early night a woman had lain in the dust against the outer wall of Maria's cook-shop. She was extremely drunk and unpleasant to look upon. Exactly when she had dropped, or been dropped there, no one knew. Porgy had not seen her when he had driven in at sunset. But he had heard some talk of her among those who had entered later. One of the men had come in laughing.

"I seen Crown's Bess outside," he said. "Must be she come aroun' tuh look fur um."

"She sho goin' tuh hab one long res', ef she goin' wait dere fur um. Dat nigger gone f'om hyuh fas' and far!" another had averred.

It was ten o'clock; and Maria was closing her shop. The great negress was in the act of fastening the window, when the tall, gaunt form of the woman lurched through the door into the faint illumination of the smoking lamp. The visitor measured the distance to the nearest bench with wandering and vacant eyes, plunged for it, and collapsed, with head and arms thrown across a table.

Maria was exasperated, but equal to the emergency. Catching the woman around the middle, she swung her easily to the door, dropped her into outer darkness, and returned to the window.

A crash caused her to turn suddenly. There was the woman again, sprawled across the table as before.

"I swear tuh Gawd!" exclaimed the provoked negress. "Ef yuh ain't de persistentes' nigger I ebber seen." She went over, lifted the woman's head, and looked into eyes in the far depths of which a human soul was flickering feebly.

"Somethin' tuh eat," the woman whispered. "Lemme hab somethin' tuh eat, an' I'll go."

Growling like an approaching equinoctial gale, Maria brought bread and fish; and emptying the dregs of the coffeepot into a cup, placed it before her.

"Now, eat an' trabble, Sister," she advised laconically.

The woman raised her head. An ugly scar marked her left cheek, and the acid of utter degradation had etched hard lines about her mouth; but eyes into which human consciousness was returning looked fearlessly into the determined face of the big negress. For a moment she ate wolfishly; then asked suddenly:

"Who lib in dat room 'cross de way?"

"Porgy," she was informed, "but such as

yuh ain't gots no use fuh he. He a cripple,
an' a beggar."

"He de man wid goat?"

"Yes, he gots goat."

The woman's eyes narrowed to dark, un-
fathomable slits.

"I hyuh say he gits good money fum de
w'ite folks," she said slowly.

In silence the meal was finished. Then
the woman steadied herself a moment with
hands against a table, and, without a word
to Maria, walked quickly, with an almost
haughty carriage, from the room.

She crossed the narrow drive with a decisive tread, opened the door of Porgy's
room, entered, and closed the door behind
her.

§

It was late afternoon. Serena Robbins
entered the court, paused at Porgy's door,
and gave a sharp rap on the weathered panel.
The door was opened by a woman. The
visitor looked through her, and spoke directly to Porgy, who sat within.

"I gots good news," she announced. "I
done been tuh see my w'ite folks 'bout
Peter; an' dey say dey gots a frien' who is
a lawyer, an' he kin git um out. I tell um

tuh sen' um tuh see you 'bout um, 'cause
yuh gots so much sense when yuh talks tuh
w'ite folks."

Having delivered her message, Serena
turned a broad back upon the woman who
stood silently in the doorway, and with the
bearing of an arbiter of social destinies,
strode to her corner of the court.

Across the drive, Maria, vast and moist,
hung over her stove in a far corner of her
cook-shop. Several negroes sat at the little
tables, eating their early suppers, laughing
and chaffing.

"Yuh sho got good-lookin' white gals in
dis town," drawled a slender young octo-
roon. He was attired in sky-blue, peg-top
trousers, yellow spats, and in the center of
a scarlet bow-tie gleamed an immense paste
horseshoe.

"Do listen tuh Sportin' Life!" said a
black, loutish buck admiringly. "Ef he
ain't lookin' at de rollin' bones, he always
gots he eye on de women."

Maria's heavy tread shook the room as
she crossed and stood, with arms akimbo,
scowling down at her iridescent guest. The
man looked up, lowered his eyes quickly,
and shifted uneasily in his chair.

"Nigger!" she finally shot at him, and the
impact almost jarred him from his chair.

"I jus' tryin' ter figger out wedder I bettuh
kill yuh decent now, wid yuh frien's about
yuh; or leabe you fuh de w'ite gentlemens
tuh hang attuh a while."

"Come now, old lady, don't talk like dese
old-fashioned lamp-oil niggers what have
had no adwantage. Why, up in New York,
where I been waitin' in a hotel—"

But he got no further.

"Noo Yo'k," she shouted. "Don't yuh
try any Noo Yo'kin' aroun' dis town. Ef I
had my way, I'd go down tuh dat Noo Yo'k
boat, an' take ebbery Gawd's nigger what
come up de gang plank wid er Joseph coat
on he back an' a glass headlight on he
buzzom and drap um tuh de catfish befo' he
foot hit decent groun'! Yas; my belly fair
ache wid dis Noo Yo'k talk. De fus t'ing
dat dem nigger fuhgit is dat dem is nigger.
Den dem comes tuh dese decent country
mens, and fills um full ob talk wut put
money in de funeral ondehtakuh pocket."
Breathless, she closed her arraignment by
bringing a fist the size of a ham down upon
the table with such force that her victim
leapt from his chair and extended an ingratiating hand toward her.

"Dat' all right, Auntie. Le's you an' me
be frien'."

"Frien' wid yuh?" and her tone dripped

scorn. "One ob dese days I might lie down wid er rattlesnake, and when dat time come, yuh kin come right along an' git intuh de bed. But till den, keep yuh shiny carcase in Noo Yo'k till de debbil ready tuh take chaage ob um!"

Suddenly the anger left her eyes, and her face became grave. She leaned over, and spoke very quietly into his face.

"Fuh Gawd's sake, don't talk dat kind ob talk tuh dese hyuh boys. Dis county ain't nebber yit see a black man git lynch. Dese nigger knows folks, an' dey knows nigger. Fer Gawd' sake keep yuh mout' off w'ite lady. Yuh gots plenty ob yuh own color fuh talk 'bout. Stick tuh dem, an' yuh ain't git inter no trouble."

During Maria's attack upon her guest, the court had been full of the many-colored sounds that accompanied its evening life. Now, gradually the noise shrunk, seeming to withdraw into itself. All knew what it meant. A white man had entered. The protective curtain of silence which the negro draws about his life when the Caucasian intrudes hung almost tangibly in the air. No one appeared to notice the visitor. Each was busily preoccupied with his task. Yet the newcomer made no move that was not noted by fifty pairs of inscrutable eyes.

The man wore a soft hat drawn well down over his face. He was slender and tall, and walked with his body carried slightly forward, like one who is used to meeting and overcoming difficulties.

A young woman passed him. He reached out and touched her on the arm. She stopped, and turned immediately toward him, her eyes lowered, her manner submissive, but utterly negative.

"I am looking for a man by the name of Porgy," he said in a clear pleasant voice. "Can you direct me to his room?"

"Porgy?" she repeated slowly, as though trying to remember. Then she called aloud: "Anybody hyuh know a man by de name ob Porgy?"

Several of the silent bystanders looked up. "Porgy?" they repeated, one after another, with shakes of the head.

The white man laughed reassuringly, as though quite used to the proceeding. "Come," he urged, "I am his friend, Mr. Alan Archdale; I know that he lives here, and I want to help him."

From behind her tubs, Serena advanced, knocking the ashes from her clay pipe as she came. When she was quite close, she stopped, and peered up into the face above her. Then she turned upon the girl.

"Go 'long an' call Porgy," she commanded. "Can't yuh tell *folks* when yuh see um?"

A light broke over the young woman's face.

"Oh, yuh means *Porgy?*" she cried, as though she had just heard the name for the first time; "I ain't understan' wut name yuh say, Boss," and echoes arose from different parts of the court. "Oh, yes, de gentleman mean *Porgy*. How come we ain't understan'." Then the tension in the air broke, and life resumed its interrupted flow.

The young woman stepped to Porgy's door, and called. Presently the door opened, and a woman helped the beggar out to his seat upon the sill, then seated herself behind him in the deep gloom of the room.

Archdale crossed the short distance, and seated himself on the sill beside the negro.

"Tell me about your friend who got locked up on account of the Robbins murder," he asked, without preamble.

In the dim light, Porgy leaned forward and looked long into the keen, kindly face of his questioner.

Archdale gave a surprised exclamation: "Why, you're the old man who used to beg in front of the apothecary shop on King Charles Street!" he said. Then, after a moment of scrutiny: "But you are not old, after all, are you?" and he studied the face intently. There was a touch of grey in the wool above the ears, and strong character lines flared downward from the nose to corners of a mouth that was, at once, full-lipped and sensuous, yet set in a resolute line most unusual in a negro. With the first indications of age upon it, the face seemed still alive with a youth that had been neither spent nor wasted.

"But, tell me about your friend," said the visitor, breaking a silence that was commencing to become tense.

Porgy's face still wore its mask. "How come yuh tuh care, Boss?" he queried.

"Why, I am the Rutledge's lawyer; and I look after their colored folks for them. I think they must have owned half the slaves in the county. A woman here, Serena Robbins, is the daughter of their old coachman, or something; and she asked them to help her friend out."

"Peter ain't gots no money, yuh know, Boss. An' I jes begs from do' to do'." There was still a shade of suspicion in Porgy's voice.

Archdale laughed reassuringly. "It will not take any money. At least, not much; and I am sure that Mrs. Rutledge will take care of that. So you can go right ahead and tell me all about it."

Fully satisfied at last, Porgy told the tale of the killing and the subsequent arrest of Peter.

When he had finished the recital, Archdale sat silent for a while. "The dirty hounds!" he said under his breath. Finally he turned wearily to Porgy, and explained slowly:

"Of course we can go to law about this; but it will take no end of time. There is an easier way. He must have someone, who is acceptable to the magistrate, to go his bond. Do you know a man by the name of Huysenberg, who keeps a corner-shop down by the West-end wharf?"

Porgy, listening intently, nodded.

Archdale handed him a bill. "Take this ten dollars to him, and tell him that you want him to go Peter's bond. He hasn't any money of his own, and his shop is in his wife's name; but he has an arrangement with the magistrate that makes him entirely satisfactory."

He handed Porgy a card with an address pencilled under a printed name. "You will find me here," he said. "If Peter is not out in two days after you hand over the ten, let me know." Then, with a brisk,

but friendly "Good night," he left the
court.

§

There was great rejoicing in Catfish Row.
Peter had returned. The ten dollar bill
which Archdale had given Porgy had
worked the miracle. Except for the fact
that the old negro's shoulders drooped, and
his grip on actualities seemed weakened by
his confinement, there was no evidence to
show that he had been absent. He had gone
to the horse-dealer, and had found his
ancient beast still awaiting a purchaser.
Another contract had been signed which had
started him off again on the eternal weekly
payment. The German had driven back
with the furniture, which Peter had docilely
purchased for the second time. Again "The
Great Emancipator" had been hung in his
accustomed place above the mantel. Now,
each morning, the old wagon rattled out
over the cobbles, with the usual number of
small, ecstatic, black bodies pendant from
its dilapidated superstructure.

"De buckra sho gots nigger figgered out
tuh a cent!" said Peter philosophically, and
even with a note of admiration in his voice.
"Dem knows how much money wagon make

in er week; an' de horse man, de furniture
man, an' de lan'lo'd mek dey 'rangement'
accordin'. But I done lib long 'nough now
tuh beat 'em all, 'cause money ain't no use
tuh a man attuh he done pass he prime,
nohow."

When the old man had settled firmly
back into his nook, and had an opportunity
to look about him, he noticed a change in
Porgy.

"I tell yuh dat nigger happy," he said
to Serena, one evening while they were
smoking their pipes together on her washing
bench.

"Go 'long wid yuh!" she retorted. "Dat
'oman ain't de kin' tuh mek man happy. It
tek a killer like Crown tuh hol' she down."

"Dat may be so," agreed the old man
sagely. "But Porgy don' know dat yit.
An' 'side, ef a man is de kin' wut needs er
'oman, he goin' be happy regahdless. Him
dress she up in he own eye till she look lak
de Queen of Sheba tuh um. Porgy t'ink
right now dat he gots a she-gawd in he
room."

"He sho' gots de kin' wut goin' gib um
hell," Serena commented cynically. "Dat
'oman ain't fit tuh 'sociate wid. Much as
I like Porgy, I wouldn't swap t'ree wo'd wid
she."

"Dat's all so, Sister," conceded Peter. "But yuh keep yo' eye on Porgy. He usen tuh hate all dese chillen. Ain't he? Now watch um. Ebery day w'en he come home he gots candy-ball fuh de crowd. An' wut mo', yistuhday I hyuh he an' she singin' tuh-gedduh in dey room."

Serena motioned to him to be quiet. Porgy's woman crossed the court to draw a bucket of water from the common tap near Serena's corner. She was neatly dressed, and passed them as though they did not exist. Filling her pail, she swung it easily to her head, and, steadying it lightly with one hand, returned close to them with an air of cool scorn that produced entirely different effects upon her two observers. Serena watched her departure in silence.

"Dat de t'ing!" said Peter, a note of admiration in his voice. "She sho ain't axin' no visit offen none of she neighbor." And he emitted an indiscreet chuckle, which was too much for his friend.

"Yuh po', ole, wall-eyed, sof'-headed gran'daddy! Ain't yuh 'shame' tuh set dey befo' me, an' talk sweet-mout' 'bout dat murderin' Crown's Bess? Ef I wuz yo' age, an' er man, I'd sabe my sof' wo'd fer de Gawd-farin' ladies."

"Ef yuh wuz my age, an' a man—" commenced Peter. He hesitated, and looked long at her with his dim, kindly eyes; then he shook his head. "No; it ain't no use. Yuh wouldn't onderstan'. Dat somet'ing shemale sense ain't goin' tuh help yuh none wid." And, still shaking his head, he knocked out his pipe, and departed in the direction of the stable, where he was presently greeted by a soft, comprehending whinny.

Bess entered Porgy's room and swung her pail of water to its place beside the new wood stove that had superseded the old, open hearth, and busied herself with preparations for supper.

Porgy was seated in a low chair near the door. He was smoking contentedly, and the odd tension that had characterized him, even in his moments of silent thought, had given place to a laxed attitude of body and an expression of well-being.

An infinitesimal negro passed with a whistle and a double shuffle.

"Look hyuh, sonny!" called Porgy.

The boy paused, hesitated, and advanced slowly. Porgy held out a large round ball, striped red and white. "How 'bout er sweet?" he said a little self-consciously. The boy took the candy, and shuffled uneasily from foot to foot.

"Dat's right," said Porgy, with a burst of sudden, warm laughter, that somehow startled the child. "Now yuh come again an' see Porgy an' Bess."

III

PART III

PORGY drove slowly down King Charles Street, and appraised the prospects for hitching and settling awhile in the narrow strip of shade against the walls of the buildings. The day was sweltering, and both cripple and goat were drooping beneath the steady pressure of the sun.

A man passed, walking briskly. Porgy at once recognized the long, easy stride, and the soft felt hat drawn rather low over the eyes. He reached out and gave a slight twist to the tail of his somnambulant animal, which resulted in a shambling trot that brought the vehicle abreast of the pedestrian. But at that moment the gentleman stopped, produced a key, and opening the door of an office, passed in without looking around.

Porgy eyed the office and its environs with evident satisfaction. The building stood very near the old apothecary shop; and between it and its neighbor to the east was an entrance way several feet in width, which breathed forth an inviting coolness from its deep shade. No one was passing at the moment. Porgy turned the head of his beast

toward the entrance, gave a sudden twist to
the tail, and drove audaciously across the
pavement, and into the retreat. Then he
hitched his wagon a few feet from the
street, and seated himself, cup in hand, at
the pavement's inner edge.

"Yuh bes' git along out of Mr. Alan'
do'way wid dat goat befo' he fin' yuh. Ain't
yuh onduhstan' gentlemen ain't likes tuh
smell goat?"

Porgy looked up and met the threatening gaze of Simon Frasier.

Frasier was a practising attorney-at-law.
He was well past fifty years of age, and his
greying wool looked very white in comparison with his uncompromisingly black skin.
He had voted the democratic ticket in the
dark period of reconstrution, when such ac-
tion on his part took no little courage, and
accordingly enjoyed the almost unlimited
toleration of the aristocracy. Without possessing the official sanction of the State for
the practice of his profession, he was, by
common consent among the lawyers, per-
mitted to represent his own people in the
police and magistrates' courts and to turn
his hand to other small legal matters into
which it was thought inadvisable to enquire
too deeply.

Porgy regarded his accuser stonily.

"Ob course gentlemen ain't likes tuh smell goat," he replied.

The door opened, and Archdale looked out. From where Porgy sat he could have touched him with his hand; yet the cripple's gaze never wavered from the face of the negro, and his expression remained unchanged. Forestalling an interruption, he hastened on, in a voice that had become mildly incredulous, as he continued, "But it can't be dat attuh knowing buckra long as yuh been know um, yuh ain't onduhstan' um any better dan tuh t'ink dey would dribe away po' cripple in de heat."

Archdale made a movement that actually crossed Porgy's line of vision; but the beggar's face gave no sign of recognition. His voice rose to a pitch of indignation:

"Yuh might be a lawyuh, an' all dat; but I ain't goin' tuh hab yuh stan' dey an' tell me dat Mistuh Archdale gots dem po' w'ite-trash ways. Ob course he don't likes de smell ob goat; but he gots er haht in he breas' fuh de po' cripple nigger."

A wry smile tugged at the corner of Archdale's mouth.

"All right, Porgy," he said, "I got it all; but, gentleman or no gentleman, I can't have a goat on my doorstep. I would not have one client left in a week."

At the sound of Archdale's voice, Porgy looked around. His entire body seemed to express amazement.

"Why, hyuh's de Boss now!" he cried. Then he turned triumphantly to the negro, and added, "Wut I done tells yuh 'bout de real quality; ain't yuh done see he say I kin stay?"

Archdale became desperate. "I did not say you could," he cried, with the manner of one who puts his foot in the crack of a closing door. "You can wait there today, as I will be in court all morning; but tomorrow you must find somewhere else."

"By tuhmorruh I goin' hab dis goat wash till yuh can't tell um from one of dem rosebush in de pahk!" Porgy assured him with an ingenuous smile. "Yuh is goin' to be mighty lubbin' of dis goat attuh a while, Boss."

"No; goats don't wash, Porgy. Away you go after today." But the power of absolute conviction was not in Archdale's voice. His foot was still in the crack; but he knew that the door was closing.

"All right, Frasier; I'll see you now about your divorce business," he said to the other negro, and showed him into the office.

Presently through an open window behind Porgy came the sound of Archdale's voice:

"All right, Frasier. Out with it. The gentleman who has come down to improve moral conditions among the negroes thinks you are a menace. He is going to have you indicted for granting divorces illegally."

In a voice very different from the one in which he had arraigned Porgy, Frasier began:

"I fin' so much nigger onsattify wid dere marriage, an' I hyuh tell ob a t'ing dey calls divorce."

"Yes?" encouraged his questioner.

"So fuh a long time now I been separate dem wid a divorce wut I mek up fuh de pu'pose. An' he go fine, Boss. I done mek too much nigger happy."

"Have you one of the papers with you?"

Silence; and then Archdale's voice again.

" 'I, Simon Frasier, hereby divorce Rachel Smalls and Columbus Devo for the charge of one dollar; signed, Simon Frasier.' Well, that is simple enough. Where did you get this seal?"

"I done buy um from de junk-shop Jew, Boss."

"Don't you know there is no such thing as divorce in this State?"

"I hyuh tell dere ain't no such t'ing fuh de w'ite folks; but de nigger need um so bad, I ain't see no reason why I can't mek up one wut sati'fy de nigger? He seem tuh work berry well, too, till dat sof' mout' gentleman come 'roun' an' onsettle all my client."

A groan floated through the window to Porgy's ears, causing him to indulge in a slow, malicious smile. Then in a pained voice the negro lawyer proceeded: "He been keepin' me alibe, Boss. An' wut mo', he keep de nigger straight. Dis gentleman say dat dey gots tuh lib tuhgedduh anyhow till dey done dead. Dat's de law, he say. But nigger ain't mek dataway. I done get um all properly moralize, and dis same gentleman tell um dat my paper ain't no mo' dan a license tuh 'dulterate. So now dey just leabe each odduh anyhow, and I ain't gets no dollar. An' now he say he goin' jail me, wut mo'!"

There was a moment of silence, then Porgy heard Archdale's voice calling a number; then: "Hello! Is that the Solicitor's office? Mr. Dennis, please."

"Oh—this is Archdale, Dennis. Yes, another negro. This time it is Frasier, you know, the divorce decree case. Yes, I have him here in my office. Look here; you have

a terrifically heavy docket this term. There
is no use taking the State's money and your
valuable time on this case."

There followed a pause; then Archdale
said hastily, "Oh, no; I am not trying anything; but he is perfectly innocent of any
deliberate wrongdoing. Yes, of course; it
would be serious if he were responsible; but
you know no one takes old Frasier seriously.
A no-bill from the grand jury would save no
end of time and trouble.

"Yes; I will guarantee that he will stop."

Porgy listened intently; and after a moment he heard Archdale say, "Thank you,"
and turn his chair toward his client. Then
he heard him address the negro.

"We are not going to lock you up this
time, Simon. But you will have to stop
divorcing your people. I have given my
word. If you do it again, snap! to jail we
both go. Do you understand?"

A relieved gasp greeted the announcement,
followed by "Gawd bless yuh, Boss!" and
a moment later Frasier stood blinking in the
white glare of the street.

Porgy looked up, and in an exact imita-
tion of Frasier's professional manner, said
testily, "Mobe on, please; mobe on. I gots
a berry perlite goat hyuh wut objec' tuh de
smell ob de jail-bird."

A chuckle sounded from Archdale's office.

Immediately the light of victory, carefully veiled, but bright, shone in Porgy's eyes. He reached behind him and tweaked the goat by the ear. The dejected animal mistook the signal, and started forward.

"No, no, bubber," whispered Porgy. "Ain't yuh hear de Boss laugh? When nigger mek de buckra laugh, den he know he done won. Dis wey we goin' spen' we libe. You watch."

§

The change in Porgy, which Peter had been the first to notice, was now apparent to all who knew him. The defensive barrier of reserve that he had built about his life was down. The long hours when he used to sit fixed and tense, with the look of introspection upon his face, were gone. Even the most skeptical of the women were beginning to admit that Bess was making him a good mate. Not that they mingled freely with the other residents of the court. On the contrary, they seemed strangely sufficient unto themselves in the midst of the intensely gregarious life that was going on about them. Porgy's earnings were adequate to their modest needs, and Bess was always up and out

with the first of the women, and among them
all there was none who could bargain more
shrewdly with the fishermen and hucksters
who sold their wares on the wharf.

Like Porgy, Bess had undergone a subtle
change that became more evident from day
to day. Her gaunt figure had rounded out,
bringing back a look of youthful comeliness,
and her face was losing its hunted expression. The air of pride that had always
shown in her bearing, which had amounted
almost to disdain, that had so infuriated the
virtuous during her evil days, was height-
ened, and, in her bettered condition forced
a resentful respect from her feminine tra-
ducers.

One morning while she was doing her
marketing on the wharf, one of the river
men who had known her in the past, hailed
her too familiarly. He was at that moment
stepping from the top round of a ladder on
to the wharf.

"How 'bout ternight?" he asked with a
leer.

She was holding a string of whiting in her
left hand, and was hanging upon the final
penny of a bargain with the fishman. She
half turned, and delivered a resounding slap
with her right hand. The man staggered
backward, hung for a moment, then van-

ished. There was a tremendous splash from the shallow water.

"Twenty cent fuh dis string, an' not one cent mo'," Bess continued coolly to the fish-man.

He accepted the price. Bess gave him eighteen cents, and a hard look. He counted the money, glanced at the hand that now hung innocently against her apron, then laughed.

"Just as yuh say, Sister. I ain't quarrelin' none wid *yuh dis* mornin'."

Bess gave him one of the faint, cryptic smiles that always made men friends and women enemies for her, and departed for Catfish Row, as if nothing had happened to break the dull routine of the morning's chores.

§

Saturday night, and the court had flung off its workaday clothes and mood. In the corner by Serena's washbench a small intimate circle had gathered about a smoking kerosene lamp. Several women sat on the bench with drowsy little negroes in their laps. A man near the light leaned over a guitar, with a vague wistfulness in his face, and plucked successive chords with a swift, running vibrance of sound. Then a deep baritone hummed for a second and raised an air:

"Ain't it hahd tuh be a nigger;
 Ain't it hahd tuh be a nigger;
 Ain't it hahd tuh be a nigger;
 'Cause yuh can't git yo' rights w'en yuh do.

"I was sleepin' on a pile ob lumber,
 Jus' as happy as uh man kin be,
 W'en a w'ite man come wake me from my
   slumber,
 An' he say, 'Yuh gots tuh work now, 'cause
   yuh free!'"

Then they were all in on the chorus:

"Ain't it hahd tuh be a nigger,"

and the gloom hummed with the low, close harmonies.

In another corner the crap circle had gathered. Porgy's delight in the game had not waned with his increasing interests, and he sat fondling the small white cubes, and whispering to them in his old confidential manner.

"Little w'ite babies," he crooned, "come sing fuh dis nigger."

He cast—and won.

Gathering the little heap of pennies and nickels, he passed them behind him to Bess, who squatted in the shadows. She took the money in silence, counted it, dropped it into her apron pocket, and continued to watch the game intently, smiling her cryptic smile when Porgy won, but saying scarcely anything at all.

The negro known as Sportin' Life had come in just as the game was commencing, and had sat in. That he was not altogether above suspicion was evidenced by the fact that the little circle of men refused to allow him to use his own dice, and told him so frankly. He scowled at them, dropped the dice back into his pocket, and started to leave. Then he seemed to think better of it, and joined the circle.

As the game proceeded it became evident that Porgy's luck was with him; he was the most consistent winner, and Sportin' Life was bearing most of the burden. But the mulatto was too good a gambler to evince any discomfiture. He talked steadily, laughed much, and missed no opportunity to drop a sly word of suspicion when Porgy drew in a pot. There was nothing that could be taken up and resented, but Porgy was mystified, and Bess' face was dark with

anger more than once. He had a way of
leaning over just as Porgy cast, and placing
his face almost on the flags so that he could
see under the dice when they struck. Then
he would look up, laugh meaningly into
Porgy's face, and sometimes clap his hands
as though the cripple had managed something very cleverly.

When the game finally broke up it was
clear that he had poisoned the minds of the
company, and the good nights lacked their
usual warmth.

Bess reached into her apron pocket, and
drew out the evening's winnings. The coins
made quite a little weight in her hand. A
late fragment of moon swung over the wall
and poured its diminished light into her
open palm. She commenced to count the
money. Porgy left her, and drew himself
into his room. She proceeded to count, absorbed in her task.

§

"Porgy lucky," said a low voice beside
her. "Mus' be yer gots two dollar dere fer
um." Sportin' Life lifted his elegant
trousers, so that the knees would not bag,
and squatted on the flags at her side. He
removed his stiff straw hat, with its bright

band, and spun it between his hands. The
moonlight was full upon his face, with its
sinister, sensuous smile.

She looked at him squarely a moment,
then said in a cold, level voice:

"I can't 'member ebber meetin' a nigger
dat I like less dan I does you."

"Thank yer kindly," he replied, not in
the least degree daunted. "But jus' de
same, I wants ter be frien' wid yer. Me
and you ain't usen ter dese small-town slow
ways. We ain't been above seein' night-life
what is night-life, an' I jus' wants ter talk
to you now and den; dat's all."

"I gots no time fuh talk," she told him.
"An' wut mo', I t'rough wid de kin' ob
nights you is t'inking 'bout."

"No mo' red-eye; none 'tall?" he queried.
"Nebber gits t'irsty, eh?"

"Yes, Gawd knows, I does git t'irsty now
and den," she said impulsively; then added
sharply, "But I done t'rough now, I tells
yer; I done t'rough."

She arose to go. "Yo' kin' mek me sick,"
she told him; "an' I ain't wants tuh hab no
mo' talk wid yuh."

He got spryly to his feet, and stood beside
her. "Oh, come on, le's let bygone be bygone, an' be frien'." Then his voice became

low and ingratiating: "Come; gimme yer han', Sister," he said.

Acquiescent, but mystified, she held out her open palm.

He poured a little pile of white powder into it. There it lay in the moonlight, very clean and white on her dark skin. "Happy dus'!" she said, and her voice was like a gasp. "Take dat t'ing away, nigger. I t'rough wid um, I tells yuh." But she did not turn her hand over and let it fall upon the ground.

"Jus' a little touch fer ole time sake," he whispered. " 'Tain't 'nough ter hurt er fly. An' it ain't goin' ter cos' yer one cent."

She stood a moment longer, and her hand trembled, spilling a few grains between her fingers. Then suddenly she clapped her palm over her mouth. When she took it away it was quite empty.

Sportin' Life heaved a sigh of relief, turned and leant against the wall—and waited.

In the corner by Serena's bench the party was breaking up. Only a few women were left, and instead of the blur of general talk, remarks leapt clear. They were discussing the crap game that had just closed.

"Dey is somet'ing berry queer 'bout de

way de money always go tuh de same place,"
a voice was saying.

The moonlight ebbed from the corner
where Bess and Sportin' Life stood. Five
minutes had passed since she had made her
sudden decisive gesture. She stood oddly
rigid, with her hands clenched at her sides.

Abruptly she spun around. "Yuh gots
mo' ob dat?" Her voice was low and taut.

"Sho' I has!" came the answer, with a
confident laugh. "But it don't come cheap.
Gimme dat money yer got dere."

Silently she held out her hand, and poured
the coins into his palm.

He gave her a small folded paper.

"I got more ob dat when yer needs it,"
he said, as he turned away.

But she did not hear him. She snatched
the paper, opened it, and threw the contents
into her mouth.

The court was sinking to sleep. One by
one the lighted windows went blank. The
women at the washbench got to their feet.
One yawned noisily, and another knocked
her clay pipe out on the flags in a shower
of sparks. Then a voice came clearly—the
one that had complained before about the
crap game.

"I ain't sayin' ef it conjer, er jus' plain
loaded dice. All I gots tuh say is dat dam

nigger, Porgy, steal my Sam' wages off him now t'ree week runnin'."

Out of the shadows and across the moon-lit square a figure flashed, gesturing wildly.

The women leapt back. The one who had done the talking screamed once, the shrill note echoing around the walls. The advancing figure closed convulsive hands upon her shoulders and snatched her body forward. Wide, red-lit eyes glared into her face. A voice half sobbed, half screamed, "Yuh say dat 'bout Porgy? Yuh say Porgy is t'ief?"

The victim was young and strong. She tore the hands from her shoulders and raised her arms before her face. One of the other women reached out to seize the intruder, but was met with a glare so insanely malignant that she retreated screaming.

Above them windows were leaping to light. Dark bodies strained from sills. Feet sounded, running down clapping dilapidated stairways. A shrill, long, terrifying shriek cut across the growing noise, and the women clinched and fell. Bystanders rushed to intervene, and became involved. Always in the centre of the storm a maddened woman whirled like a dervish and called horribly upon her God, striking and clawing wildly.

The babel became terrific. The entire

population of the court contributed to the
general confusion. In the rooms above, children wailed out a nameless terror.

Suddenly over the tumult sounded the
gong of the patrol wagon, and through the
gateway half-a-dozen policemen advanced
with pistols out, and clubs ready.

The uproar stopped suddenly at its peak.
Shadows dropped back and were gulped by
deeper shadow. Feet made no sound in retreating. Solid bodies became fluid, sliding.
Yawning doorways drew them in. Miraculously the court was converted into a vacant,
walled square, in which stood six erect figures, looking a little theatrical and foolish
with their revolvers and clubs, and a woman
who shook menacing hands at nothing at all
and swore huskily at phantoms.

"No trouble finding the cause of the disturbance," said an authoritative voice. "Get
her, men. Better use bracelets. Can't tell
about dope cases."

The squad closed quickly. For a moment
a grotesque shadow tumbled and shifted in
the centre of the court; then a voice said,
"Steady now." The mass broke into individual figures, and, under the ebbing moonlight, moved toward the entrance with a
manacled woman in their midst.

Porgy had opened his door at the first outcry and sat on the sill trying to get the import of the disturbance. Now, as the group passed close to him, he looked up. The woman had ceased her outcry, and was looking about with vague, unseeing eyes. As they walked past his doorway, so close that he could have touched the nearest officer with his hand, she looked down, and her gaze focussed upon the sitting figure. Her body stiffened, and her head lifted with the old, incongruous gesture of disdain.

"Bess!" called Porgy once very loudly; and again, in a voice that sagged, "Bess!"

One of the policemen paused and looked down upon the speaker. But the woman turned deliberately away, and he hastened to rejoin the party. Then the wagon clanged down the darkened street.

§

Under the gas light that supplemented a far, dusty window in the Recorder's Court, stood Bess. She swayed, and her face twitched ocasionally; but her glance was level, and her head erect.

Behind a high desk sat a man well past middle age. His florid complexion caused his long grey mustache to appear very white. His eyes were far apart and suggested a kindness that was born of indolence, rather than of wide compassion. His hands were slender and beautifully made, and he sat with elbows on desk, and finger-tips touching. When he spoke it was in a drawl that suggested weariness.

"What is the charge, Officer?" he asked.

"Bein' under the influence of dope, an' creatin' a disturbance in Catfish Row, yer Honor," replied the policeman who stood by the prisoner.

"Anybody hurt?"

"Not as we was able to see, yer Honor."

The judge turned to the prisoner.

"Have you ever been here before?"

"No, suh," came the reply in a low, clear tone.

"The officer of the day thinks she has, yer Honor," put in the policeman, "but he can't swear to it. She looks like a hundred others, he says, scar and all; an' they change names so fast you get nothing from the records."

The judge regarded the prisoner with amiability. The thermometer on the wall beside him registered ninety. It was asking too much of good-nature to require it to subvert itself in such heat.

"I suppose we will have to give you the

benefit of the doubt," he said. Then he turned to the officer.

"After all, it's the man who sold her the poison we want. I was kept here three hours yesterday by dope cases. I want it put a stop to."

He contracted his brows in a weak attempt at sternness, and directed a steady gaze at Bess.

"Who sold you that dope?"

She met his eyes squarely.

"I don't t'ink I know um again," she said in a low, even tone. "I buy from um in de dark, las' night, an' he gone off right away."

"It's no use, Your Honor," put in the policeman. "They won't give each other away."

The judge fixed the culprit with a long scrutiny. Then he asked:

"Have you any money to pay a fine?"

"No, suh. Yuh'll jus' hab tuh gib' me my time."

A man entered the room.

"I beg your pardon, Your Honor," he said, "but there is a cripple outside in a goat-cart who says he is prepared to pay the woman's fine."

"Eh; what's that?" exclaimed the judge. "Is it that black scoundrel, Porgy, the beggar?"

"That's him, Yer Honor," replied the man, with a grin.

"Why, the highwayman takes a dime from me every time I venture on King Charles Street. And here he has the audacity to come and offer to pay a fine."

"Don't tek he money, Boss."

The prisoner said the words steadily, then caught her lower lip with her strong, white teeth.

"Address the Court as 'Your Honor,' not 'Boss,'" ordered the judge.

"Yo' Honuh," amended the culprit.

For a long moment the Recorder sat, his brow contracted. Then he drew a large, cool, linen handkerchief from his pocket and mopped his face.

"Go out and take ten dollars from the beggar," he told the policeman. "It's a small fine for the offence." Then turning to the woman, he said:

"I am going to lock you up for ten days; but any time you give the name of that dope peddler to the jailor you can leave. Do you understand?"

Bess had nothing to say in reply, and after a moment the policeman took her by the arm.

"This way to the wagon," he directed, and led her from the court room.

The street was a blaze of early morning sun, and the woman covered her eyes with her hand. The wagon stood, step to curb, and the officer hurried her across the narrow pavement and into the conveyance.

The bell clanged, and the heavy horse flung its weight against the collar.

Something impelled Bess to remove her hand and to look down.

Below the high side of the patrol, looking rather like a harbor tug beside an ocean liner, stood the goat-cart. For a moment she looked into Porgy's face. It told her nothing, except that he seemed suddenly to have grown older, and that the real Porgy, who had looked out at her from the eyes for a little while, had gone back into his secret places and closed the door.

The wagon lunged forward.

Then Porgy spoke.

"How long?" he called.

The incessant clamor of the gong commenced, and the hoofs beat their noisy tattoo upon the stones.

Bess raised both hands with fingers extended.

The wagon rounded a corner and disappeared.

§

The jail in which Bess was incarcerated was no better, and no worse, than many others of its period, and the score of negro women with whom she found herself could not be said to suffer acutely under their imprisonment. When life reaches a certain level of misery, it envelopes itself in a protective anesthesia which deadens the senses to extremes; and having no tasks to perform, the prisoners awaited the expiration of their brief sentences with sodden patience, or hastened the passage of time with song.

By day they were at liberty to exercise in the jail yard, a square of about half an acre surrounded by a high brick wall, containing not so much as a single blade of grass. Like a great basin, the yard caught and held the heat which poured from the August sun until it seemed to overflow the rim, and quiver, as though the immense vessel had been jarred from without. But the soaring walls gave always a narrow strip of shade to which the prisoners clung, moving around the sides as the day advanced, with the accuracy of the hand of a sundial.

Before nightfall the prisoners were herded into the steaming interior of the building, and Bess and the other women were locked in a steel cage, which resembled a large dog-pound and stood in the centre

of a high, square room, with a passageway
around it. A peculiarly offensive moisture
clung to the ceiling, and streamed in little
rivulets down the walls. An almost un-
breatheable stench clogged the atmosphere.

The jailers were not vindictive. They
were not even unkind. Some of them evidenced a mild affection for their charges,
and would pause to exchange greetings with
them on their rounds. But it would have
meant effort to better the living conditions,
and effort on the part of a white warden in
August was not to be considered. They
locked them up, gave them a sufficiency of
hominy and white pork to sustain life,
allowed them to see their visitors, talk, and
sing to their heart's content. If they were
suffering from tuberculosis, or one of a hundred nameless and communicable diseases,
when they entered, it was none of the
County's affair. And if they left showing
that ash-pallor so unmistakable in a negro,
it was as lamentable as it was unavoidable.
But when all was said and done, what must
one expect if one added to the handicap of
a dark skin the indiscretion of swallowing
cocaine and indulging in a crap game?

Bess received but one visitor during her
imprisonment. When the callers were ad-

mitted, on the day following her arrival,
Maria loomed in the centre of the small,
timid group. She went directly to Bess
where she sat by the wall, with her eyes
closed against the glare. The big negress
wore an expression of solicitude, and her
voice was low and surprisingly gentle as she
said:

"Porgy ask me tuh bring yer dis blanket
fuh lie on, an' dese fish an' bread. How
yuh is feelin' now?" Then she bent over
and placed a bundle in the prisoner's lap.

Bess opened her eyes in surprise.

"I ain't been expectin' no fabors off none
ob you folks," she replied. "How come yuh
tuh care ef I lib er die, attuh dat row I
mek?"

Maria lowered herself to a seat beside her.

"I lubs dat nigger, Porgy, lak he been my
chile," she told her. "An' wut mo', I t'ink
I know what done happen tuh yuh."

"Wut yuh know?"

"I been in my do' dat night; an' I seen dat
skunk, Sportin' Life, sell yuh dat stuff. Ef
I had er known den wut it wuz, I'd a been
hyuh long side ob yuh now fuh murder."

After a moment, she asked: "Wut mek
yuh don't tell de jailluh who done um, an'
come on home?"

Bess remained silent for a moment; then

she raised her head and looked into the eyes
of the older woman.

"I's a 'oman grown. Ef I tek dope, dat
muh own business. Ef I ebber gits muh han'
on dat nigger, I goin' fix um so he own
mammy ain't know um! But I ain't goin'
gib um 'way tuh de w'ite folks."

The hard lines about her mouth softened,
and, in scarcely more than a whisper, she
added:

"I gots tuh be decent 'bout somet'ing, 'less
I couldn't go back an' look in Porgy face."

Maria got heavily to her feet. The other
visitors were leaving, and she longed to be
free of the high, brick walls. She dropped a
hand on Bess's shoulder.

"Yuh do right, Sister. But ef dat yalluh
nigger come tuh Catfish Row agin—leabe
him fuh me—dat's all!" Then the big
negress joined the departing group, and
passed out through the small steel doorway
that pierced the massive gate.

Bess sat for a long while without moving.
The sun lifted over the high wall, and drove
its white-hot tide into her lap, and upon
her folded hands.

"Wut mek yuh ain't mobe intuh de
shade?" a neighbor asked curiously.

Bess looked up and smiled.

"I jes' settin' hyuh t'inkin' 'bout muh

frien'," she said. "Yuh done hear um call
me 'Sister,' ain't yuh? Berry well den.
Dat mean me and she is frien'."

§

Bess lay upon the bed in Porgy's room
and stared at the ceiling with hard, bright
eyes. From time to time she would pluck
at the sheet that covered her and utter hurried, indistinct sentences that bore not the
slightest relation to existing circumstances.
A week had passed since her release, and its
seven interminable days had been spent in
this fashion.

Porgy was out upon the day's rounds.
Occasionally the door to the sick-room would
open, and an awed, black face peer in. The
mystery of delirium frightened and per-
plexed the negroes, and limited the manifes-
tations of kindness and sympathy that they
usually bestowed upon unfortunate friends.
Even Maria was not proof against this
dread, and the irrelevant observations that
greeted her when she went in with the daily
lunch sent her hurrying wide-eyed from the
room.

Porgy returned early in the evening. His
face was deeply marked, but the lines were
those of anxiety, and his characteristic firm-

ness of mouth and jaw was gone. He closed
the door on the curious glances of his neigh-
bors, and lifted himself to a seat upon the
bed.

"How Bess now?" he asked softly.

She shifted her gaze from the ceiling to
his face.

"Eighteen miles tuh Kittiwar!" she mut-
tered. "Rattlesnake', palmettuh bush, an'
such."

Her eyes were suddenly fearful, and she
closed her hand tightly upon his.

Porgy cast a hurried glance over his shoulder. Then, reassured, stroked her brow, and
comforted her in his deep, gentle voice.

"Yuh hyuh wid Porgy now; an' nuttin'
can't hurt yuh. Soon de cool wedder comin'
an' chill off dese febers. Ain't yuh 'member
how dat cool win' come tuh town wid de
smell ob pine tree; an' how de star is all
polish up lak w'ite folks' silber? Den
ebbery body git well. Ain't yuh know?
Yuh jus' keep still, an' watch wut Porgy
say."

She was silent after that, and closed her
eyes. Presently, to his relief, he saw that
she was sleeping. This was the moment for
which he had been waiting. He went out,
closing the door very gently, and joined a
group of sympathisers in the court.

"Wut we goin' do now?" he asked. "A week gone, an' she ain't none better."

Peter knocked out his clay pipe on a flagstone, with three staccato little raps, thus gaining the attention of the circle.

"Ef yuh wants tuh listen tuh me," he remarked weightily, "I adwise yer tuh sen' she tuh de w'ite folk' hospital."

His words were received with a surprise amounting to incredulity.

"Fuh Gawd sake, Daddy Peter!" an awed voice said at last. "Ain't yuh knows dey lets nigger die dey, so dey kin gib um tuh de student?"

But the old negro stood his ground.

"De student ain't gits um 'til he done dead. Ain't dat so? Den he can't hurt um none. Ain't dat so, too? An' I gots dis tuh say. One ob my w'ite folks is er nuss tuh de hospital; and dat lady is er pure angel wid de sick nigger. Ef I sick tuhmorruh I goin' tuh she; an' wut she say is good wid me. I wants dis carcase tek care ob w'ile he is alibe. W'en he done dead, I ain't keer."

"Yuh ain't keer whedder yuh is cut up an' scatter, 'stead of bein' bury in Gawd own grabe-yahd?" someone asked the iconoclast.

Under this direct attack, the old man weakened.

"Well, mebbe I ain't sayin' I jus' as lief,"

he compromised. "But I t'ink Gawd onduhstan' de succumstance, an' mek allowance."

Serena Robbins broke the silence which
followed.

"How come yuh ain't ax me fuh pray ober
um?" she enquired in a slightly offended
voice. "Mus' be yuh is done fergit how
Gawd done answer we las' prayeh, and sen'
dat goat tuh sabe yu' life, when starbation
done stan' dey an' look yuh in de eye."

Porgy brightened at that, and turned
eagerly from the dark horror of Peter's suggestion.

"Dat so, my Sister," he commenced; but
her eyes were already closed, and her body
was swaying from side to side, as she sat
cross-legged on the flags. Presently she
began to intone:

"Oh, Jedus, who done trouble de wateh in
de sea ob Gallerie—"

"Amen!" came the chorus, led by Porgy.

"An' likewise who done cas' de Debbil out
ob de afflicted, time an' time agin—"

"Oh, Jedus!"

"Wut mek yuh ain't lay yo' han' on dis
sister' head?"

"Oh, my fadder!"

"An' sen' de Debbil out ob she, down er
steep place intuh de sea, lak yuh use' tuh do,
time an' time agin?"

"Time an' time agin!"

"Ain't dis po' cripple done lif' up out de dus' by we prayeh?"

"Da's de trut', Jedus."

"Eben so, lif' up he woman, an' mek she well, time an' time agin!"

"Time an' time ag'in! Allelujah!"

After the prayer the group scattered, each going silently away in the late dusk, until there remained only Porgy, who sat with bowed head, and Maria, massive and inscrutable, beside him.

When the last retreating footstep died away, the great negress bent her turbaned head over until it almost touched Porgy's face.

"Listen tuh me," she whispered. "Yuh wants dat 'oman cure up; ain't yuh?"

"Yuh knows I does." And, already suffering from the reaction from religious enthusiasm, his voice was flat and hopeless.

"Berry well den. De ribber boat leabe fum de wharf at sebben o'clock, tuhmorruh mo'nin'. Yuh knows dat deck-han' by de name Mingo?"

Porgy nodded assent, his eyes intent upon her face.

"Well; git on de wharf early, an' gib um two dollar. Tell um w'en de boat done git tuh Ediwander Islan' at eight tuhmorruh night, tuh go right tuh Lody cabin, an' tell she tuh mek a conjer tuh cas' de debbil out Bess."

"Yuh t'ink dat cure she?" asked Porgy, with a glimmer of new hope in his eyes.

"I ain't t'ink. I knows," came in tones of absolute conviction. "Now, min'; an' do wut I say."

The big negress shuffled away to her room, leaving Porgy alone in the gloom.

The bent, solitary figure raised its eyes to the square of sky, with its bewildering profusion of stars, that fitted like a lid over the high rim of the court. There were no sounds except a weary land breeze that fingered the lichens on the south wall, and a whisper from the bay, as the tide lifted its row of shells and pebbles a notch further up the littered beach.

Now that all human companionship had been withdrawn, the watcher felt strangely alone, and smaller than the farthest star or most diminutive shell. Like a caged squirrel, his tired mind spun the rounds of his three alternatives: First, the white man's science, gaunt, clean, and mysterious, with the complete and awful magistracy which it assumed over the luckless bodies that fell into its possession. He knew that it returned some healed in body. He knew that others had passed into its portals, and had been obliterated utterly. Then his second alternative: the white man's God, vague and abstract as the wind that moved among the lichens, with his Jesus, who could stir him suddenly to his most beautiful songs and make his heart expand until, for a moment, it embraced all mankind with compassionate love, but who passed, as the wind passes, leaving him cold and disillusioned. One of these he must choose, or else turn his face back to the old blurred trail that receded, down, down, down to the beginning of things: to the symbols one might hold, tangible and terrifying; to the presciences that shuddered like dawn at the back of the brain and told one what to do without the process of thought.

As though bent beneath a great physical weight, Porgy sat without moving, until the pattern on his glittering ceiling had changed and shifted. Then he lifted his face slowly, drew his sleeve across his moist forehead, and entered his room.

§

Just before sunrise Porgy left his room and hitched up his goat. In the upper air over Catfish Row a single buzzard hung poised. Slowly it careened to a current of air, and its belly and under-wings lit to a ruddy glory from the sun, which was still below the horizon. Porgy saw it and winced. But as he went about his task there was no indecision in his face. He harnessed the goat with steady hands, drove out of the court and to the pier-head.

He experienced no difficulty in finding his man. Mingo accepted the mission and the handful of pennies and nickels; and Porgy, having closed the bargain, returned at once to the court.

Maria was opening her shop as he entered, and paused with a shutter in her hands. She could scarcely believe her eyes. The beggar's face was bright, and he was humming a tune.

"Wut de news?" she asked. "Bess done git well?"

"Not jus' yit," he replied. "But I done had me a dream las' night; an' de dream say tuh sen' tuh de conjer 'oman; an' Bess goin' break she feber tuhnight."

"Da's right, my Brudder," Maria responded heartily. "Dat 'oman good as well now. You watch!"

All day, sitting by Archdale's office, Porgy hummed his tune, and counted off the hours of the steamboat's voyage. Now she would be passing Kittiwar, and, in only a few hours more, she would be coming to rest for the night at Ediwander.

The counting off continued after he went to bed, and he was strangely undisturbed by Bess's mutterings. Now the boat had arrived, he finally told himself. Maria had said that the cabin was near the landing. Surely it would not take the woman long to brew the spell. His excitement increased to a mood of exaltation. He lay with his hand upon Bess's forehead, waiting.

Far away St. Christopher struck the hour. The mellow bells threw the quarter hours out like a handful of small gold coins to ring down upon the drowsy streets. Then, very deliberately, they dropped ten round, heavy notes into the silence.

This should be the moment. Porgy pressed his hand harder, and sweat broke out upon his brow. For a moment it seemed to him that life hung suspended.

"Porgy," said a weak, flat voice beside him. "Porgy, dat you dey, ain't it? Why you ain't talk tuh me?"

The cripple's answer was a sudden high laugh that broke to a sob.

"T'ank Gawd!" he said; and again, "T'ank Gawd!"

§

On the evening following the day upon which Bess had taken her turn for the better, Maria was alone in her shop. The supper hour was over, and her patrons had departed. She was busy at her stove, and did not turn immediately when someone entered. When she finally looked over her shoulder, her customer had buried his face in his hands, and she failed to recognize him. Of one fact there could be little doubt: the man was drunk, for the close, little room was already heavy with the exhalations of vile corn whiskey.

She crossed the room, and touched the man on the shoulder. He lowered his hands and attempted to focus his eyes on her face.

"Oh, it's you, Mingo?" she said, and even then she did not grasp the significance of his presence in the city at that time.

"Gimme some supper," he growled; and, with an uncertain movement, drew some change from his pocket and spilled it in a small pile on the table.

Maria looked at the money. There was about half a dollar in all, but there were only two nickels, and the remainder was in pennies. It looked suspiciously like the currency in which Porgy paid his debts. Then, as she stood looking down at the little heap

of copper, the full import of the man's presence dawned upon her.

"Wut yuh doin' here now?" she demanded of him in a tense whisper; "when
de ribber boat ain't due back fuh annoder
day?"

The question stirred her customer's consciousness to a faint gleam of life; but it did
not vitalize it sufficiently for adroit prevari-
cation.

"I miss de boat dis trip," he managed to
articulate. "I take er drink wid er frien',
and when I git tuh de wharf, de boat done
gone."

Two powerful hands gripped his shoulders and flung him back against the wall.
He opened his eyes wide and looked into a
face of such cold ferocity that his loose lips
emitted a sudden "Oh, Jedus!" and he became immediately sober, and very much
afraid.

Then Maria poured into his ears words
that had the heat and dead weight of molten
lead.

"Now I goin' lock yuh up in dat closet
till de ribber boat is back at de wharf," she
concluded. "Den I goin' let yuh loose. But
I all de time goin' be where I kin git my
hand on yuh again. Ef yuh ebber tells
Porgy, or any libbin' soul, dat yuh ain't de-

liber dat message tuh Lody, I goin' tuh hab nigger blood on my soul w'en I stan' at de jedgement. Now yuh gots dat straight in yuh head?"

Mingo nodded assent. He was beyond the power to speak.

The big negress jerked him suddenly to his feet, propelled him across the room and into the stygian recesses of the closet. Then she slammed the door, turned the immense iron key in the lock, and dropped it in her pocket.

"Well, dat's dat!" she remarked, as she wiped a moist, mystified face upon a corner of her apron. "Mus' hab been Jedus done um atter all." Then, as though to dismiss the matter, she added: "No, I be damn ef he did. He ain't gots it in um."

IV

PART IV

IT was the day set for the grand parade
and picnic of "The Sons and Daughters
of Repent Ye Saith the Lord," and, with
the first light of morning, Catfish Row had
burst into a fever of preparation. Across
the narrow street, the wharf, from which the
party was to leave, bustled and seethed with
life. A wagon rattled out to the pier-head
and discharged an entire load of watermelons. Under the vigilant eyes of a committee a dozen volunteers lifted the precious
freight from the vehicle, and piled it ready
for the steamer.

From behind the next pier, with a frenzied
threshing of its immense stern paddle, came
the excursion boat. Tall open exhaust fun-
nels flanked the walking-beam, and coughed
great salmon-colored plumes of steam into
the faint young sunlight. A fierce torrent
of wood-smoke gushed from the funnel and
went tumbling away across the harbor.
Painters were hurled, missed, coiled, and
hurled again. Then, amid a babblement of
advice and encouragement, the craft was
finally moored in readiness for the Lodge.

The first horizontal rays of the sun were painting the wall a warm claret, when Porgy opened his door, to find Peter already dressed for the parade, and perched upon the back of his gaily blanketed horse. He wore a sky-blue coat, white pants which were thrust into high black leggings, and a visored cap, from beneath which he scowled fiercely down upon the turmoil around the feet of his mount. Across his breast, from right shoulder to left hip, was a broad scarlet sash, upon which was emblazoned, "Repent Ye Saith the Lord!" and from his left breast fluttered a white ribbon bearing the word "MARSHAL." From time to time, he would issue orders in hoarse, menacing gutturals, which no one heeded; and twice, in the space of half an hour, he rode out to the pier-head, counted the watermelons, and returned to report the number to an important official who had arrived in a carriage to supervise the arrangements.

Momently the confusion increased, until at eight o'clock it culminated in a general exodus toward the rendezvous for the parade.

The drowsy old city had scarcely commenced its day when, down through King Charles Street, the procession took its way. Superbly unselfconscious of the effect that

it produced, it crashed through the slow, re-
strained rhythm of the city's life like a wild,
barbaric chord. All of the stately mansions
along the way were servantless that day, and
the aristocratic matrons broke the ultimate
canon of the social code and peered through
front windows at the procession as it swept
flamboyantly across the town.

First came an infinitesimal negro boy,
scarlet-coated, and aglitter with brass but-
tons. Upon his head was balanced an enormous shako; and while he marched with left
hand on hip and shoulders back, his right
hand twirled a heavy gold-headed baton.
Then the band, two score boys attired in
several variations of the band master's costume, strode by. Bare, splay feet padded
upon the cobbles; heads were thrown back,
with lips to instruments that glittered in the
sunshine, launching daring and independent excursions into the realm of sound.
Yet these improvisations returned always to
the eternal boom, boom, boom of an under-
lying rhythm, and met with others in the
sudden weaving and ravelling of amazing
chords. An ecstasy of wild young bodies
beat living into the blasts that shook the
windows of the solemn houses. Broad,
dusty, blue-black feet shuffled and danced
on the many-colored cobbles and the grass

between them. The sun lifted suddenly over the housetops and flashed like a torrent of warm, white wine between the staid buildings, to break on flashing teeth and laughing eyes.

After the band came the men members of the lodge, stepping it out to the urge of the marshals who rode beside them, reinforcing the marching rhythm with a series of staccato grunts, shot with crisp, military precision from under their visored caps. Breast cross-slashed with the emblems of their lodge, they passed.

Then came the carriages, and suddenly the narrow street hummed and bloomed like a tropic garden. Six to a carriage sat the sisters. The effect produced by the colors was strangely like that wrought in the music; scarlet, purple, orange, flamingo, emerald; wild, clashing, unbelievable discords; yet, in their steady flow before the eye, possessing a strange, dominant rhythm that reconciled them to each other and made them unalterably right. The senses reached blindly out for a reason. There was none. They intoxicated, they maddened, and finally they passed, seeming to pull every ray of color from the dun buildings, leaving the sunlight sane, flat, dead.

For its one brief moment out of the year

the pageant had lasted. Out of its fetters of
civilization this people had risen, suddenly,
amazingly. Exotic as the Congo, and still
able to abandon themselves utterly to the
wild joy of fantastic play, they had taken
the reticent, old Anglo-Saxon town and
stamped their mood swiftly and indelibly
into its heart. Then they passed, leaving
behind them a wistful envy among those
who had watched them go,—those whom the
ages had rendered old and wise.

§

When the exodus from the Row was completed, Bess helped Porgy out to the boat
and established him in an angle of the main-
deck cabin, where he could see and enjoy
the excursion to the full. Below them on
the wharf, Maria, who had the direction of
the refreshment committee in hand, moved
about among the baskets and boxes, looking rather like a water-front conflagration,
in a voluminous costume of scarlet and
orange. Bess left Porgy and descended the
ladder.

"I gots a ready hand wid bundle," she
announced diffidently.

The immense negress paused, and looked
her up and down.

"Well, well, it looks like yer tryin' ter be decent," she commented.

Instantly the woman chilled. "Yuh kin go tuh Hell!" she said deliberately. "I ain't axin' fuh no sermon. I want a job. Does yuh want a han' wid dem package, or not?"

For a moment their eyes met. Then they laughed suddenly, loudly together, with complete understanding.

"All right, den," the older woman said. "Ef yuh is dat independent, yuh kin tek dem basket on board."

After that they worked together, until the procession arrived, without the interchange of further remarks.

§

Down the quiet bay, like a great, frenzied beetle, the stern-wheeler kicked its way. On the main deck the band played without cessation. In a ring before it, a number of negroes danced, for the most part shuffling singly. The sun hurled the full power of an August noon upon the oil-smooth water, and the polished surface cast it upward with added force under the awnings. The decks sagged with color, and repeated explosions of laughter rode the heat waves back to the drowsing, lovely old city long after the boat had turned the first bend in the narrow river and passed from view on its way to the negro picnic grounds on Kittiwar Island.

Thrashing its way between far-sweeping marshes and wooded sea islands, the boat would burst suddenly into lagoon after lagoon, that lay strewn along the coast, that blazed in the noon like great fire-opals held in silver mesh.

Finally a shout went up. Kittiwar lay before them, thrusting a slender wharf from its thickly wooded extremity into the slack tide.

The debarkation over, Maria took possession of a clearing that stood in a dense forest of palmettoes and fronted on the beach, and marshalled her committee to prepare the lunch. From the adjacent beach came the steady, cool thunder of the sea and the unremitting hum of sand, as tireless winds scooped it from the dunes and sent it in low, flat-blown layers across the hard floor of the beach.

The picnickers heard it, and answered with a shout. Soon the streaming whiteness of the inner surf was dotted with small, glistening black bodies; the larger figures, with skirts hoisted high, were wading in the shallows.

Porgy sat with a large myrtle bush in

one hand, with which he brushed flies from several sleeping infants. The sun lay heavy and comforting upon him. One of the children stirred and whimpered. He hummed a low, bumbling song to it. There was a new contentment in his face. After a while he commenced to nod.

§

"I go an' git some palmettuh leaf fuh tablecloth," Bess told Maria; and, without waiting for an answer, she took a knife from a basket, and entered the dense tangle of palm and vine that walled the clearing.

Almost immediately she was in another world. The sounds behind her became faint, and died. A rattler moved its thick body sluggishly out of her way. A flock of wood ibis sprang suddenly up, broke through the thick roof of palm leaves, and streamed away over the treetops toward the marsh with their legs at the trail.

She cut a wide fan-shaped leaf from the nearest palmetto. Behind her some one breathed—a deep interminable breath.

The woman's body stiffened slowly. Her eyes half closed and were suddenly dark and knowing. Some deep ebb or flow of blood touched her face, causing it to darken heavily, leaving the scar livid. Without turning, she said slowly:

"Crown!"

"Yas, yuh know berry well, dis Crown."

The deep sound shook her. She turned like one dazed, and looked him up and down.

His body was naked to the waist, and the blue cotton pants that he had worn on the night of the killing had frayed away to his knees. He bent slightly forward. The great muscles of his torso flickered and ran like the flank of a horse. His small wicked eyes burned, and he moistened his heavy lips.

Earth had cared for him well. The marshes had provided eggs of wild fowl, and many young birds. The creek had given him fish, crabs and oysters in abundance, and the forest had fed him with its many berries, and succulent palmetto cabbage.

"I seen yuh land," he said, "an' I been waitin' fuh yuh. I mos' dead ob lonesome on dis damn island, wid not one Gawd's person to swap a word wid. Yuh gots any happy-dus' wid yuh?"

"No," she said; then with an effort, "Crown, I gots somethin' tuh tell yuh. I done gib up dope; and beside dat, I sort ob change my way."

His jaw shot forward, and the huge shoulder muscles bulged and set. His two great hands went around her throat and closed like the slow fusing of steel on steel. She stopped speaking. He drew her to him until his face touched hers. Under his hands her arteries pounded, sending fierce spurts of flame through her limbs, beating redly behind her eyeballs. His hands slackened. Her face changed, her lips opened, but she said nothing. Crown broke into low, shaken laughter, and threw her from him.

"Now come wid me," he ordered.

Into the depths of the jungle they plunged; the woman walking in front with a trance-like fixity of gaze. They followed one of the narrow hard-packed trails that had been beaten by the wild hogs and goats that roamed the island.

On each side of them, the forest stood like a wall, its tough low trees and thick-bodied palmettoes laced and bound together with wire-strong vines. Overhead the foliage met, making the trail a tunnel as inescapable as though it had been built of masonry.

The man walked with a swinging, effortless stride, but his breath sounded in long, audible inhalations, as though he labored physically.

When they had journeyed for half an hour they crossed a small cypress swamp. The cypress-knees jutted grotesquely from the yellow water, and trailing Spanish moss extended drab stalactites that brushed their faces as they threaded the low, muddy trail.

Finally Bess emerged into a small clearing, in the centre of which stood a low hut with sides of plaited twigs and roof of palmetto leaves laid on top of each other in regular rows like shingles.

Crown was close behind her. At the low door of the hut she paused and turned toward him. He laughed suddenly and hotly at what he saw in her face.

"I know yuh ain't change," he said. "Wid yuh an' me it always goin' tuh be de same. See?"

He snatched her body toward him with such force that her breath was forced from her in a sharp gasp. Then she inhaled deeply, threw back her head, and sent a wild laugh out against the walls of the clearing.

Crown swung her about and threw her face forward into the hut.

§

The sun was so low that its level rays shot through the tunnels of the forest and

bronzed its ceiling of woven leaves when
Bess returned to the clearing. She paused
for a moment. Behind her, screened by the
underbrush, stood Crown.

"Now 'member wut I tells yuh," he said.
"Yuh kin stay wid de cripple 'til de cotton
come. Den I comin'. Davy will hide we
on de ribber boat fur as Sawannah. Den
soon de cotton will be comin' in fas', an'
libbin will be easy. Yuh gits dat?"

For a moment she looked into the narrow,
menacing eyes, then nodded.

"Go 'long den, an' tote fair, les yuh wants
tuh meet yo' Gawd."

She stepped into the open. Already most
of the party were on the boat. She crossed
the narrow beach to the wharf.

Maria stood by the gangplank and looked
at her with suspicious eyes. "Wuh yuh been
all day?" she demanded.

"I git los' in de woods, an' I can't git my
bearin's 'til sundown. But dat ain't nobody' business 'cep' me an' Porgy, ef yuh
wants tuh know."

She found Porgy on the lower deck near
the stern, and seated herself by him in
silence. He was looking into the sunset, and
gave no evidence of having noticed her
arrival.

Through the illimitable, mysterious

night, the steamer took its way. Presently it swung out of one of the narrow channels and wallowed like an antediluvian monster into the stillness of a wide lagoon. Out of the darkness, low, broad waves moved in upon it, trailing stars along their swarthy backs to shatter into silver dust against the uncouth bows.

To Porgy and Bess, still sitting silent in the stern, came only the echoes of drowsy conversations, sounds of sleeping, and the rhythmic splash and drip of the single great wheel behind them. The boat forged out into the centre of the lagoon, and the shore line melted out behind it. Where it had shown a moment before, could now be seen only the steady climb of constellations out of the water's rim, and the soft, humid lamps of low, near stars. The night pressed in about the two quiet figures.

Porgy had said no word since their departure. His body had assumed its old, tense attitude. His face wore again its listening look. Now, he said slowly:

"Yuh nebber lie tuh me, Bess."

"No," came an even, colorless voice, "I nebber lie tuh yuh. Yuh gots tuh gib me dat."

Another interval, then:

"War it Crown?"

A sharp, indrawn breath beside him, and a whisper:

"How yuh know?"

"Gawd gib cripple many t'ings he ain't gib strong men." Then again, patiently, "War it Crown?"

"Yes, it war."

"Wut he say?"

"He comin' fuh me when de cotton come tuh town."

"Yuh goin'?"

"I tell um—yes."

After a while the woman reached out a hand and closed it lightly about the man's arm. Under the sleeve she felt the muscles go rigid. What power! She tried to circle it with her hand. It was almost as big as Crown's. It was strange that she had not noticed that before. She opened her mouth to speak, but no sound came. Presently she sighed, and withdrew her hand.

Through the immense emptiness of sea and sky the boat forged slowly toward the distant city's lights.

§

"I gots er feelin' yistuhday," announced Maria to Serena Robbins, as she took a batch of wet clothing from the latter's tub, gave it

one twist with her enormous hands, and set
it aside to go upon the line.

"Wut yuh gots er feelin' 'bout?"

"I gots er feelin' w'en Porgy 'oman come
out de wood on de picnic, she done been wid
Crown."

At the mention of the murderer's name
Serena stepped back, and her usual expression of sanctimonious complacency slowly
changed. Her lower lip shot forward, and
her face darkened.

"Yuh t'ink dat nigger on Kittiwar?" she
asked.

"I allus figgered he bin dey in dem deep
palmetters," Maria replied. "But w'en I
look in Bess's eye las' night, I sho ob two
t'ing: one, dat he is dey, an' two, dat she
been wid um."

"Yuh b'lieb she still run wid dat nigger?"

"Dem sort ob mens ain't need tuh worry
'bout habin' 'omen," Maria told her. "Dey
kin lay de lash on um, an' kick um in de
street; den dey kin whistle w'en dey ready,
an' dere dey is ag'in lickin' dey han'."

"She goin' stay wid Porgy, ef she know
wut good fuh she."

"She know all right, an' she lub Porgy.
But ef dat nigger come attuh she, dey ain't
goin' tuh be noboddy roun' hyuh but Porgy
an' de goat."

A sudden dark flame blazed in Serena's face, sweeping the acquired complacency before it, and changing it utterly. She leant forward, and spoke heavily:

"Dat nigger bes' t'ank he Gawd dat I gots My Jedus now fuh hol' back my han'!"

"Yuh ain't means dat yuh is goin' tuh gib um up tuh de w'ite folks ef he come back to town, 'stead ob settle wid um yu'self?" Maria asked incredulously.

"I ain't know wut fuh do," the other replied, the hatred in her face giving way to a look of perplexity. "Ef dat nigger come tuh town he sho tuh git kill' sooner er later. Den de w'ite folks goin' lock me up. Dey gots it on de writin's now dat I been Robbins' wife; an' dey goin' figger I like as not kill um. I knows two people git lock up dat way, an' dey ain't do one Gawd t'ing."

"Nigger sho' gots fuh keep he eye open in dis worl'," the big negress observed. "But we can't turn no nigger ober tuh de police."

A man paused before the entrance of the court, and looked in. To the two women he was only a silhouette standing under the arch against a dazzling expanse of bay; but the foppish outlines of the indolent, slender figure were unmistakable.

A smile of pleased anticipation grew about

Maria's wide mouth. She dried her hands upon her apron.

"Jus' like I been tellin' yuh!" she remarked to Serena. "T'ank Gawd, Jedus ain't gots me yit wuh he gots you; an' I still mens enough tuh straighten out a crooked nigger. See dat yalluh snake wrigglin' in de do'way? He de one wut sell Bess dat happy-dus'."

Drying her hands and bared forearms with ominous thoroughness, she crossed to her shop. The room was empty when she entered. She went at once to the stove which stood in its corner, with its legs set upon four bricks. She bent forward, placed a shoulder against one of its corners, gave a heave, and drew out a brick. Then she straightened up, spat first on one hand, then on the other, and, carrying the brick in her immense right, lightly, and with a certain awful fondness, stepped out of her door.

Sportin' Life was now within the entrance, and presented an unsuspecting profile to the cook-shop.

With frightful deliberation, Maria swung her long arm back; then, like the stroke of a rattler, it shot forward. The brick caught the mulatto full on the side of the head. He crumpled among his gaudy habiliments like a stricken bird.

After a space of time the victim blinked
feebly, then opened his eyes upon Maria's
face. She was mopping his head with a
wet rag, and his first glance discovered an
expression of gentleness on her heavy fea-
tures. Reassured, he opened his eyes wide.
But the gentleness was gone. He felt himself gripped by the shoulders, and suddenly
snatched upward to be placed upon unsteady
legs. Then he was propelled rapidly toward
the gate.

At the pavement's edge Maria swung her
victim around until his wandering and re-
luctant gaze met hers.

"De las' time yuh wuz aroun' hyuh, I
ain't hab nuttin' on yuh but my eyes. Now
I knows yuh—yuh damn, dirty, dope-ped-
dler, wreckin' de homes ob dese happy
niggers!"

Her arms shot forward and back like loco-
motive pistons. The man's head snapped
to an acute angle, and righted itself with
difficulty.

"Now, w'en I done flingin' yuh out dis
gate," she proceeded, "it's de las' time yuh
is goin' tuh leabe it erlibe. Eberybody say
I is er berry t'orough nigger, an' ef yuh ebber
comes roun' hyuh agin, drunk or sobuh, I
ain't goin' to be t'rough wid yuh carcase

ontil I t'row yuh bones out tuh de buzza'd
one by one."

Abruptly she reversed the luckless man
and placed a foot in the small of his back.
Then with a heave that seemed to bring into
play every muscle of her huge bulk, she
catapulted him once and for all out of Catfish Row and the lives of its inhabitants.

V

PART V

"FISH runnin' well outside de bar, dese days," remarked Jake one evening to several of his seagoing companions.

A large, bronze-colored negro paused in his task of rigging a line, and cast an eye to sea through the driveway.

"An' we mens bes' make de mores ob it," he observed. "Dem Septumbuh storm due soon, an' fish ain't likes eas' win' an' muddy watuh."

Jake laughed reassuringly.

"Go 'long wid yuh. Ain't yuh done know we hab one stiff gale las' summer, an' he nebber come two yeah han' runnin'."

His wife came toward him with a baby in her arms, and, giving him the child to hold, took up the mess of fish which he was cleaning in a leisurely fashion.

"Ef yuh ain't mans enough tuh clean fish no fastuh dan dat, yuh bes' min' de baby, an' gib um tuh a 'oman fuh clean!" she said scornfully, as she bore away the pan.

The group laughed at that, Jake's somewhat shamefaced merriment rising above the others. He rocked the contented little negro

in his strong arms, and followed the retreating figure of the mother with admiring
eyes.

"All right, mens," he said, returning to
the matter in hand. "I'm all fuh ridin' luck
fer as he will tote me. Turn out at fo' tuhmorruh mornin', and we'll push de 'Seagull'
clean tuh de blackfish banks befo' we wets
de anchor. I gots er feelin' in my bones dat
we goin' be gunnels undeh wid de pure fish
when we comes in tuhmorruh night."

The news of Jake's prediction spread
through the negro quarter. Other crews got
their boats hastily in commission and were
ready to join the "Mosquito Fleet" when it
put to sea.

On the following morning, when the sun
rose out of the Atlantic, the thirty or forty
small vessels were mere specks teetering
upon the water's rim against the red disc
that forged swiftly up beyond them.

Afternoon found the wharf crowded with
women and children, who laughed and joked
each other as to the respective merits of their
men and the luck of the boats in which they
went to sea.

Clara, Jake's wife, sought the head of the
dock long before sundown, and sat upon the
bulkhead with her baby asleep in her lap.
Occasionally she would exchange a greeting

with an acquaintance; but for the most part
she gazed toward the harbor mouth and said
no word to any one.

"She always like dat," a neighbor informed a little group. "A conjer 'oman once
tell she Jake goin' git drownded; an' she
ain't hab no happiness since, 'cept when he
feet is hittin' de dirt."

Presently a murmur arose among the
watchers. Out at the harbor mouth, against
the thin greenish-blue of the horizon, appeared the "Mosquito Fleet." Driven by a
steady breeze, the boats swept toward the
city with astonishing rapidity.

Warm sunlight flooded out of the west,
touched the old city with transient glory,
then cascaded over the tossing surface of
the bay to paint the taut, cupped sails
salmon pink, as the fleet drove forward directly into the eye of the sun.

Almost before the crowd realized it, the
boats were jibing and coming about at their
feet, each jockeying for a favorable berth.

Under the skillful and daring hand of
Jake, the "Seagull" took a chance, missed a
stern by a hairbreadth, jibed suddenly with
a snap and boom, and ran in, directly under
the old rock steps of the wharf.

A cheer went up from the crowd. Never
had there been such a catch. The boat

seemed floored with silver which rose almost
to the thwarts, forcing the crew to sit on
gunnels, or aft with the steersman.

Indeed the catch was so heavy that as
boat after boat docked, it became evident
that the market was glutted, and the fishermen vied with each other in giving away
their surplus cargo, so that they would not
have to throw it overboard.

§

By the following morning the weather
had become unsettled. The wind was still
coming out of the west; but a low, solid wall
of cloud had replaced the promising sunset
of the evening before, and from time to time
the wind would wrench off a section of the
black mass, and volley it with great speed
across the sky, to accumulate in unstable
pyramids against the sunrise.

But the success of the day before had so
fired the enthusiasm of the fishermen that
they were not easily to be deterred from following their luck, and the first grey premoni-
tion of the day found the wharf seething
with preparation.

Clara, with the baby in her arms, accompanied Jake to the pier-head. She knew the
futility of remonstrance; but her eyes were

fearful when the heavy, black clouds swept overhead. Once, when a wave slapped a pile, and threw a handful of spray in her face, she moaned and looked up at the big negro by her side. But Jake was full of the business in hand, and besides, he was growing a little impatient at his wife's incessant plea that he sell his share of the "Seagull" and settle on land. Now he turned from her, and shouted:

"All right, mens!"

He bestowed a short, powerful embrace upon his wife, with his eyes looking over her shoulder into the Atlantic's veiled face, turned from her with a quick, nervous movement, and dropped from the wharf into his boat.

Standing in the bow, he moistened his finger in his mouth, and held it up to the wind.

"You mens bes' git all de fish yuh kin tuhday," he admonished. "Win' be in de eas' by tuhmorruh. It gots dat wet tas' ter um now."

One by one the boats shoved off, and lay in the stream while they adjusted their spritsails and rigged their full jibs abeam, like spinnakers, for the free run to sea. The vessels were similar in design, the larger ones attaining a length of thirty-five feet. They were very narrow, and low in the waist, with high, keen bows, and pointed sterns. The hulls were round-bottomed, and had beautiful running lines, the fishermen, who were also the designers and builders, taking great pride in the speed and style of their respective craft. The boats were all open from stem to stern and were equipped with thole-pins for rowing, an expedient to which the men resorted only in dire emergency.

Custom had reduced adventure to commonplace; yet it was inconceivable that men could put out, in the face of unsettled weather, for a point beyond sight of land, and exhibit no uneasiness or fear. Yet bursts of loud, loose laughter, and snatches of song, blew back to the wharf long after the boats were in mid-stream.

The wind continued to come in sudden flaws, and, once the little craft had gotten clear of the wharves, the fleet made swift but erratic progress. There were moments when they would seem to mark time upon the choppy waters of the bay; then suddenly a flaw would bear down on them, whipping the water as it came, and, filling the sails, would fairly lift the slender bows as it drove them forward.

By the time that the leisurely old city was sitting down to its breakfast, the fleet had disappeared into the horizon, and the sun had climbed over its obstructions to flood the harbor with reassuring light.

The mercurial spirits of the negroes rose with the genial warmth. Forebodings were forgotten. Even Clara sang a lighter air as she rocked the baby upon her lap.

But the sun had just lifted over the eastern wall, and the heat of noon was beginning to vibrate in the court, when suddenly the air of security was shattered. From the center of town sounded the deep, ominous clang of a bell.

At its first stroke life in Catfish Row was paralyzed. Women stopped their tasks, and, not realizing what they did, clasped each others' hands tightly, and stood motionless, with strained, listening faces.

Twenty times the great hammer fell, sending the deep, full notes out across the city that was holding its breath and counting them as they came.

"Twenty!" said Clara, when it had ceased to shake the air.

She ran to the entrance and looked to the north. Almost at the end of vision, between two buildings, could be seen the flagstaff that surmounted the custom-house. It was bare when she looked—just a thin, bare line against the intense blue, but even as she stood there, a flicker of color soared up its length; then fixed and flattened, showing a red square with a black center.

"My Gawd!" she called over her shoulder. "It's de trut'. Dat's de hurricane signal on top de custom-house."

Bess came from her room, and stood close to the terrified woman.

"Dat can't be so," she said comfortingly. "Ain't yuh 'member de las' hurricane, how it tek two day tuh blow up. Now de sun out bright, an' de cloud all gone."

But Clara gave no sign of having heard her.

"Come on in!" urged Bess. "Ef yuh don't start tuh git yuh dinner, yuh won't hab nuttin' ready fuh de mens w'en dey gits in."

After a moment the idea penetrated, and the half-dazed woman turned toward Bess, her eyes pleading.

"You come wid me, an' talk a lot. I ain't likes tuh be all alone now."

"Sho' I will," replied the other comfortingly. "I min' de baby fuh yuh, an' yuh kin be gittin' de dinner."

Clara's face quivered; but she turned from the sight of the far red flag and opened her door for Bess to pass in.

After the two women had remained together for half an hour, Bess left the room

for a moment to fetch some sewing. The
sun was gone, and the sky presented a
smooth, leaden surface. She closed the door
quickly so that Clara might not see the
abrupt change, and went out of the entrance
for a look to sea.

Like the sky, the bay had undergone a
complete metamorphosis. The water was
black, and strangely lifeless. Thin, intensely white crests rode the low, pointed
waves; and between the opposing planes of
sky and sea a thin westerly wind roamed
about like a trapped thing and whined in a
complaining treble key. A singularly clear
half-light pervaded the world, and in it she
could see the harbor mouth distinctly, as
it lay ten miles away between the north and
south jetties that stretched on the horizon
like arms with the finger-tips nearly touching.

Her eyes sought the narrow opening.
Guiltless of the smallest speck, it let upon
utter void.

"It'd take 'em t'ree hour tuh mek harbor
from de banks wid good win'," said a
woman who was also watching. "But dere
ain't no powuh in dis breeze, an' it a head
one at dat."

"Dey kin row it in dat time," encouraged
Bess. "An' de storm ain't hyuh yit."

But the woman hugged her forebodings, and stood there shivering in the close, warm air.

§

Except for the faint moan of the wind, the town and harbor lay in a silence that was like held breath.

Many negroes came to the wharf, passed out to the pier-head, and sat quietly watching the entrance to the bay.

At one o'clock the tension snapped. As though it had been awaiting St. Christopher's chimes to announce "Zero Hour," the wind swung into the east, and its voice dropped an octave, and changed its quality. Instead of the complaining whine, a grave, sustained note came in from the Atlantic, with an undertone of alarming variations, that sounded oddly out of place as it traversed the inert waters of the bay.

The tide was at the last of the ebb, and racing out of the many rivers and creeks toward the sea. All morning the west wind had driven it smoothly before it. But now, the stiffening eastern gale threw its weight against the water, and the conflict immediately filled the bay with large waves that leapt up to angry points, then dropped back sullenly upon themselves.

"Choppy water," observed a very old negro who squinted through half-closed eyes. "Dem boat nebbuh mek headway in dat sea."

But he was not encouraged to continue by the silent, anxious group.

Slowly the threatening undertone of the wind grew louder. Then, as though a curtain had been lowered across the harbor mouth, everything beyond was blotted by a milky screen.

"Oh, my Jedus!" a voice shrilled. "Here he come, now! Le's we go!"

Many of the watchers broke for the cover of buildings across the street. Some of those whose men were in the fleet crowded into the small wharf-house. Several voices started to pray at once, and were immediately drowned in the rising clamor of the wind.

With the mathematical precision that it had exhibited in starting, the gale now moved its obliterating curtain through the jetties, and thrust it forward in a straight line across the outer bay.

There was something utterly terrifying about the studied manner in which the hurricane proceeded about its business. It clicked off its moves like an automaton. It was Destiny working nakedly for the eyes of men

to see. The watchers knew that for at least
twenty-four hours it would stay, moving its
tides and winds here and there with that in-
vincible precision, crushing the life from
those whom its preconceived plan had
seemed to mark for death.

With that instant emotional release that
is the great solace of the negro, the tightly
packed wharf-house burst into a babblement
of weeping and prayer.

The curtain advanced to the inner bay
and narrowed the world to the city, with
its buildings cowering white and fearful, and
the remaining semi-circle of the harbor.

And now from the opaque surface of the
screen came a persistent roar that was neither
of wind or water, but the articulate cry of
the storm itself. The curtain shot forward
again and became a wall, grey and impenetrable, that sunk its foundations into the
tortured sea and bore the leaden sky upon
its soaring top.

The noise became deafening. The narrow strip of water that was left before the
wharves seemed to shrink away. The buildings huddled closer and waited.

Then it crossed the strip, and smote the
city.

From the roofs came the sound as though
ton after ton of ore had been dumped from

some great eminence. There was a dead weight to the shocks that could not conceivably be delivered by so unsubstantial a substance as air, yet which was the wind itself, lifting abruptly to enormous heights, then hurling its full force downward.

These shocks followed the demoniac plan, occurring at exact intervals, and were succeeded by prying fingers, as fluid as ether, as hard as steel, that felt for cracks in roofs and windows.

One could no longer say with certainty, "This which I breathe is air, and this upon which I stand is earth." The storm had possessed itself of the city and made it its own. Tangibles and intangibles alike were whirled in a mad, inextricable nebula.

The waves that moved upon the bay could be dimly discerned for a little distance. They were turgid, yellow, and naked; for the moment they lifted a crest, the wind snatched it and dispersed it, with the rain, into the warm semi-fluid atmosphere with which it delivered its attack upon the panic-stricken city.

Notch by notch the velocity increased. The concussions upon the roofs became louder, and the prying fingers commenced to gain a purchase, worrying small holes into large ones. Here and there the wind would get beneath the tin, roll it up suddenly, whirl it from a building like a sheet of paper, and send it thundering and crashing down a deserted street.

Again it would gain entrance to a room through a broken window, and, exerting its explosive force to the full, would blow all of the other windows outward, and commence work upon the walls from within.

It was impossible to walk upon the street. At the first shock of the storm, the little group of negroes who had sought shelter in the wharf-house fled to the Row. Even then, the force of the attack had been so great that only by bending double and clinging together were they able to resist the onslaughts and traverse the narrow street.

Porgy and Bess sat in their room. The slats had been taken from the bed and nailed across the window, and the mattress, bundled into a corner, had been pre-empted by the goat. Bess sat wrapped in her own thoughts, apparently unmoved by the demoniac din without. Porgy's look was one of wonder, not unmixed with fear, as he peered into the outer world between two of the slats. The goat, blessed with an utter lack of imagination, revelled in the comfort and intimacy of his new environment, expressing his contentment in suffocating waves, after the manner of his kind. A kerosene lamp without a chimney, smoking straight up into the unnatural stillness of the room, cast a faint, yellow light about it, but only accentuated the heavy gloom of the corners.

From where Porgy sat, he could catch glimpses of what lay beyond the window. There would come occasional moments when the floor of the storm would be lifted by a burrowing wind, and he would see the high, naked breakers racing under the sullen pall of spume and rain.

Once he saw a derelict go by. The vessel was a small river sloop, with its rigging blown clean out. A man was clinging to the tiller. One wave, larger than its fellows, submerged the little boat, and when it wallowed to the surface again, the man was gone, and the tiller was kicking wildly.

"Oh, my Jedus, hab a little pity!" the watcher moaned under his breath.

Later, a roof went by.

Porgy heard it coming, even above the sound of the attack upon the Row, and it filled him with awe and dread. He turned and looked at Bess, and was reassured to see that she met his gaze fearlessly. Down the street the roar advanced, growing nearer and louder momentarily. Surely it would be the

final instrument of destruction. He held his
breath, and waited. Then it thundered past
his narrow sphere of vision. Rolled loosely,
it loomed to the second story windows, and
flapped and tore at the buildings as it swept
over the cobbles.

When a voice could be heard again, Porgy
turned to his companion.

"You an' me, Bess," he said with conviction. "We *sho'* is a little somet'ing attuh
all."

After that, they sat long without exchang-
ing a word. Then Porgy looked out of the
window and noticed that the quality of
the atmosphere was becoming denser. The
spume lifted for a moment, and he could
scarcely see the tormented bay.

"I t'ink it mus' be mos' night," he observed. "Dey ain't much light now on de
outside ob dis storm."

He looked again before the curtain descended, and what he saw caused his heart
to miss a beat.

He knew that the tide should be again at
the ebb, for the flood had commenced just
after the storm broke. But as he looked,
the water, which was already higher than
a normal flood, lifted over the far edge of
the street, and three tremendous waves broke
in rapid succession, sending the deep layers

of water across the narrow way to splash
against the wall of the building.

This reversal of nature's law struck terror
into the dark places of Porgy's soul. He
beckoned to Bess, his fascinated eyes upon
the advancing waves.

She bent down and peered into the gloom.
"Oh, yes," she remarked in a flat tone.
"It been dis way in de las' great storm. De
win' hol' de watuh in de jetty mout' so he
can't go out. Den he pile up annoder tide
on him."

Suddenly an enormous breaker loomed
over the backs of its shattered and retreating
fellows. The two watchers could not see its
crest, for it towered into, and was absorbed
by, the low-hanging atmosphere. Yellow,
smooth, and with a perpendicular, slightly
concave front, it flashed across the street,
and smote the solid wall of the Row. They
heard it roar like a mill-race through the
drive, and flatten, hissing in the court. Then
they turned, and saw their own door give
slightly to the pressure, and a dark flood
spurt beneath it, and debouch upon the
floor.

Bess took immediate command of the sit-
uation. She threw an arm about Porgy, and
hurried him to the door. She withdrew the
bolt, and the flimsy panels shot inward.

The court was almost totally dark. One after another now the waves were hurtling through the drive and impounding in the walled square.

The night was full of moving figures, and cries of fear; while, out of the upper dark, the wind struck savagely downward.

With a powerful swing, Bess got Porgy to a stairway that providentially opened near their room, and, leaving him to make his way up alone, she rushed back, and was soon at his heels with an armful of belongings.

They sought refuge in what had been the great ball-room of the mansion, a square, high-ceilinged room on the second story, which was occupied by a large and prosperous family. There were many refugees there before them. In the faint light cast by several lanterns, the indestructible beauty of the apartment was evident, while the defacing effects of a century were absorbed in shadow. The noble open fireplace, the tall, slender mantel, with its Grecian frieze and intricate scrollwork, the high panelled walls were all there. And then, huddled in little groups on the floor, or seated against the walls, with eyes wide in the lantern-shine, the black, fear-stricken faces.

Like the ultimate disintegration of a civilization—there it was; and upon it, as though to make quick work of the last, tragic chapter, the scourging wrath of the Gods—white, and black.

§

The night that settled down upon Catfish Row was one of nameless horror to the inhabitants, most of whom were huddled on the second floor in order to avoid the sea from beneath, and deafening assaults upon the roof above their heads.

With the obliteration of vision, sound assumed an exaggerated significance, and the voice of the gale, which had seemed by day only a great roar, broke up in the dark into its various parts. Human voices seemed to cry in it; and there were moments when it sniffed and moaned at the windows.

Once, during a silence in the room, a whinny was distinctly heard.

"Dat my ole horse!" wailed Peter. "He done dead in he stall now, an' dat he woice goin' by. Oh, my Gawd!"

They all wailed out at that; and Porgy, remembering his goat, whimpered and turned his face to the wall.

Then someone started to sing:

"I gots uh home in de rock, don't yuh see?"

With a feeling of infinite relief, Porgy turned to his Jesus. It was not a charm that he sought now for the assuaging of some physical ill, but a benign power, vaster perhaps even than the hurricane. He lifted his rich baritone above the others:

> "Oh, between de eart' an' sky,
> I kin see my Sabior die.
> I gots uh home in de rock,
> Don't yuh see!"

Then they were all in it, heart and soul. Those who had fallen into a fitful sleep, awoke, rubbed their eyes, and sang.

Hour after hour dragged heavily past. Outside, the storm worked its will upon the defenceless city. But in the great ball-room of Catfish Row, forty souls sat wrapped in an invulnerable garment. They swayed and patted, and poured their griefs and fears into a rhythm that never missed a beat, which swept the hours behind it into oblivion, and that finally sang up the faint grey light that penetrated the storm, and told them that it was again day.

§

At about an hour after daybreak the first
lull came. Like the other moves of the hurricane, it arrived without warning. One moment the tumult was at its height. The
next, there was utter suspension. Abruptly,
like an indrawn breath, the wind sucked back
upon itself, leaving an aching vacuum in its
place. Then from the inundated water-
front arose the sound of the receding flood.

The ebb-tide was again overdue, and with
the second tide piled upon it, the whole im-
measurable weight of the wind was required
to maintain its height. Now, with the pressure removed, it turned and raced beneath
the low-lying mist toward the sea, carrying
its pitiful loot upon its back.

To the huddled figures in the great room
of the Row came the welcome sound, as the
court emptied itself into the street. The
negroes crowded to the windows, and peered
between the barricades at the world without.

The water receded with incredible speed.
Submerged wreckage lifted above the surface. The street became the bed of a
cataract that foamed and boiled on its rush
to the sea. Presently the wharf emerged,
and at its end even a substantial remnant
of the house could be descried. How it had
survived that long was one of the inex-
plicable mysteries of the storm.

Suddenly Peter, who was at one of the windows, gave a cry, and the other negroes crowded about him to peer out.

The sea was still running high, and as a large wave lifted above the level of the others, it thrust into view the hull of a half-submerged boat. Before the watchers could see, the wave dropped its burden into a trough, but the old man showed them where to look, and presently a big roller caught it up, and swung it, bow on, for all to see. There was a flash of scarlet gunnel, and, beneath it, a bright blue bird with open wings.

"De 'Seagull'!" cried a dozen voices together. "My Gawd! dat Jake' boat!"

All night Clara had sat in a corner of the room with the baby in her arms, saying no word to anyone. She was so still that she seemed to be asleep, with her head upon her breast. But once, when Bess had gone and looked into her face, she had seen her eyes, wide and bright with pain.

Now the unfortunate woman heard the voices, and sprang to the window just in time to see the craft swoop into a hollow at the head of the pier.

She did not scream out. For a moment she did not even speak. Then she spun around on Bess with the dawn of a wild hope in her dark face.

"Tek care ob dis baby 'til I gits back," she said, as she thrust the child almost savagely into Bess's arms. Then she rushed from the room.

The watchers at the window saw her cross the street, splashing wildly through the knee-deep water. Then she ran the length of the wharf, and disappeared behind the sheltering wall of the house.

It was so sudden, and tired wits move slowly. Several minutes had passed before it occurred to anyone to go with her. Finally Peter turned from the window.

"Dat 'oman ain't ought tuh be out dey by sheself," he said. "Who goin' out dey wid me, now?"

One of the men volunteered, and they started for the door.

A sound like the detonation of a cannon shook the building to its foundations. The gale had returned, smashing straight downward from some incredible height to which it had lifted during the lull.

The men turned and looked at one another.

Shock followed shock in rapid succession. Those who stood by the windows felt them give inward, and instinctively threw their weight against the frames. The explosions merged into a steady roar of sound that surpassed anything that had yet occurred. The room became so dark that they could no longer see one another. The barricaded windows were vaguely discernible in bars of muddy grey and black. Deeply rooted walls swung from the blows, and then settled slowly back on the recoil.

A confused sound of praying filled the room. And above it shrilled the terror of the women.

For an appreciable space of time the spasm lasted. Then, slowly, as though by the gradual withdrawing of a lever, the vehemence of the attack abated. The muddy grey bars at the windows became lighter, and some of the more courageous of the negroes peered out.

The wharf could be seen dimly extending under the low floor of spume and mist. The breakers were higher than at any previous time, but instead of smashing in upon the shore, they raced straight up the river and paralleled the city. As each one swung by it went clean over the wharf, obliterating it for the duration of its passage.

Suddenly from the direction of the lower harbor a tremendous mass appeared, showing first only a vast distorted stain against the grey fabric of the mist. Then a gigantic wave took it, and drove it into fuller view.

"Great Gawd A'mighty!" some one whispered. "It's dat big lumbuh schooner bruck loose in de harbor."

The wave hunched its mighty shoulders under the vessel and swung it up—up, for an interminable moment. The soaring bowsprit lifted until it was lost in mist. Tons of water gushed from the steep incline of the deck, and poured over the smooth, black wall of the side, as it reared half out of the sea. Then the wave swept aft, and the bow descended in a swift, deadly plunge.

A crashing of timbers followed that could be heard clearly above the roaring of the storm. The hull had fallen directly across the middle of the wharf. There was one cataclysmic moment when the whole view seemed to disintegrate. The huge timbers of the wharf up-ended, and were washed out like straws. The schooner rolled half over, and her three masts crashed down with their rigging. The shock burst the lashings of the vessel's deck load, and as the hull heeled, an avalanche of heavy timbers took the water. The ruin was utter.

Heavy and obliterating, the mist closed down again.

Bess turned from the window holding the sleeping infant in her arms, raised her eyes and looked full at Porgy.

With an expression of awe in his face, the cripple reached out a timid hand and touched the baby's cheek.

§

The windows of the great ball-room were open to the sky, and beyond them, a busy breeze was blowing across its washed and polished expanse, gathering cloud-remnants into little heaps, and sweeping them in tumbling haste out over the threshold of the sea.

Most of the refugees had returned to their rooms, where sounds of busy salvaging could be heard. Porgy's voice arose jubilantly announcing that the goat had been discovered, marooned upon the cook-stove; and that Peter's old horse had belied his whinny, and was none the worse for a thorough wetting.

Serena Robbins paused before Bess, who was gathering her things preparatory to leaving the room, placed her hands upon her hips, and looked down upon her.

"Now, wut we all goin' do wid dis po' mudderless chile?" she said, addressing the room at large.

The other occupants of the room gathered behind Serena, but there was something about Bess's look that held them quiet.

They stood there waiting and saying nothing.

Slowly Bess straightened up, her face lowered and pressed against that of the sleeping child. Then she raised her eyes and met the gaze of the complacent older woman.

What Serena saw there was not so much the old defiance that she had expected, as it was an inflexible determination, and, behind it, a new-born element in the woman that rendered the scarred visage incandescent. She stepped back, and lowered her eyes.

Bess strained the child to her breast with an elemental intensity of possession, and spoke in a low, deep voice that vested her words with sombre meaning.

"Is Clara come back a'ready, since she dead, an' say somet'ing 'bout 'we' tuh yuh 'bout dis chile?"

She put the question to the group, her eyes taking in the circle of faces as she spoke.

There was no response; and at the suggestion of a possible return of the dead, the circle drew together instinctively.

"Berry well den," said Bess solemnly. "Ontell she do, I goin' stan' on she las' libbin' word an' keep dis chile fuh she 'til she do come back."

Serena was hopelessly beaten, and she knew it.

"Oh, berry well," she capitulated. "All I been goin' tuh do wuz jus' tuh puhwide um wid er propuh Christian raisin'. But ef she done gib um tuh yuh, dere ain't nuttin mo' I kin do, I guess."

VI

PART VI

OCTOBER blew down from the north, bracing, and frosty-clear. It sent a breeze racing like mad over the bay and bouncing into the court to toss the clothes-lines like lanyards of signal flags. The torpid city and wide, slumbrous marshes were stung to sudden life and laughed up at the far, crisp blue of the sky.

Out in the harbor mouth, a faint wisp of smoke grew and blackened, and presently beneath it the rusty hull of a tramp lifted from the Atlantic, and thrust its blunt nose into the waters of the bay.

Summer had gone. Soon the cotton would be coming through.

It was nine o'clock, and still Porgy lingered in the court. His blood leapt swiftly in his veins, and he experienced that sweet upsurge of life that the North knows with the bursting of spring, but that comes most keenly to the sultry lands with the strong breath of autumn. Yet, when he looked up at the sky, a vague prescience of disaster darkened his spirit. He sat beside Bess in the doorway, with his eyes upon the child in her lap.   After a while he took the baby into his arms, and then the foreboding suddenly became pain.

He looked up and met the gaze of the woman.   It was there in her eyes also, plain for him to see.

Out in the silence of the street a sound commenced to grow.   Only a faint, far murmur at first, it gathered weight until it became a steady rumble, with a staccato clip, clip, clip running through it.

There were a few women and children about, and they ran to the entrance to see. But Porgy and Bess sat and looked fixedly at the bay, where it lay beyond the gate.

Then the drays came, and the bay was blotted out by the procession.

The great mules, fat and strong from their summer in pasture, moved swiftly with a sharp click of shoes, and the drivers cracked their whips and laughed down at the crowd.   The low platforms of the vehicles seemed almost to brush the ground; and, upon them, clear to the top of the entrance arch, the bales towered, with the fibre showing in dazzling white patches where the bagging was torn.   Twenty or more in the train they passed.

Scarcely had the rumble receded in the distance, than a burst of heavy laughter sounded in the street, and two tall figures strode through the entrance and into the group of women and children. There was a bright flash from bandanas, and one of the men swung a child to his shoulder. Loud greetings followed, and another burst of laughter, heavy, deep-chested and glad.

From an upper window a woman's voice called, "Come on, Sister; le's we go down. De stevedore is comin' back."

Porgy turned toward Bess, and moistened his lips with his tongue. Then he spoke in a low husky voice:

"Us ain't talk much sence de picnic, Bess, you an' me. But I gots tuh talk now. I gots tuh know how you an' me stan'."

Bess regarded him dumbly. For a moment the look which Serena had seen when she had tried to take the baby brushed her face, then it passed, leaving it hopeless.

Porgy leaned forward. "Yuh is wantin' tuh go wid Crown w'en he come?"

Then she answered: "W'en I tek dat dope, I know den dat I ain't yo' kin'. An' w'en Crown put he han' on me dat day, I run tuh he like water. Some day dope comin' agin. An' some day Crown goin' put he han' on my t'roat. It goin' be like dyin' den. But I gots tuh talk de trut' tuh yuh. W'en dem time come, I goin' tuh go."

"Ef dey warn't no Crown?" Porgy whispered. Then before she could answer, he hurried on: "Ef dey wuz only jes' de baby an' Porgy, wut den?"

The odd incandescence flared in her face, touching it with something eternal and beautiful beyond the power of human flesh to convey. She took the child from Porgy with a hungry, enfolding gesture. Then her composure broke.

"Oh, fuh Gawd sake, Porgy, don't let dat man come an' handle me! Ef yuh is willin' tuh keep me, den lemme stay. Ef he jus' don't put dem hot han' on me, I kin be good, I kin 'member, I kin be happy."

She broke off abruptly, and hid her face against that of the child.

Porgy patted her arm. "Yuh ain't needs tuh be 'fraid," he assured her. "Ain't yuh gots yo' man? Ain't yuh gots Porgy? Wut kin' of a nigger yuh t'inks yuh gots anyway, fuh let annuduh nigger carry he 'oman? No, suh! yuh gots yo' man now; yuh gots Porgy."

§

From behind a sea island the full October moon lifted its chill disc and strewed the bay with cold, white fire. The lights were out in Catfish Row, except for a shaft of firelight that fell across the dark from Serena's room, and a faint flicker in the cook-shop, where Maria was getting her fire laid in readiness for the early breakfast.

A cry sounded in the court, which was quickly muffled; then followed low, insolent laughter.

Maria was at her door instantly. Across the court, a man could be seen for one moment, seated on Serena's wash-bench; then behind him the door closed with a bang, shutting off the shaft of firelight.

Maria crossed the court, and when she had reached the man's side he looked up. The moonlight fell upon his face. It was Crown.

"What yuh doin' hyuh?" she asked him.

"Jus' droppin' in on a few ole frien'."

"Come tuh de shop," she commanded. "I gots tuh hab talk wid yuh."

He arose obediently, and followed her.

Maria turned up the lamp and faced about as Crown entered the room. He had to bend his head to pass under the lintel, and his shoulders brushed the sides of the opening.

The big negress stood for a long moment looking at him. Her gaze took in the straight legs with their springing thighs straining the fabric of the cotton pants, the slender waist, and the almost unbelievable outward flare of the chest to the high, straight span of the shoulders.

A look of deep sadness grew in her somber face.

"Wid uh body like dat!" she said at last, "why yuh is goin' aroun' huntin' fuh deat'?"

Crown laughed uneasily, stepped into the room, and sat at a table. He placed his elbows upon it, hunched his shoulders forward with a writhing of muscle beneath the shirt, then dropped his chin in his hands, and regarded the woman.

"I know dese hyuh niggers," he replied. "Dey is a decent lot. Dey wouldn't gib no nigger away tuh de w'ite folks."

"Dat de Gawd' trut'. Only dey is odder way ob settlin' up er debt."

"Serena?" he asked, with a sidelong look, and a laugh. "Dat sister gots de fear ob Gawd in she heart. I ain't 'fraid none ob she."

After a moment of silence he asked abruptly:

"Bess still libbin' wid de cripple?"

"Yes; an' she a happy, decent 'oman. Yuh bes' leabe she alone."

"Fer Gawd' sake! Wut yuh t'ink I come tuh dis damn town fuh? I ain't jus' huntin' fuh deat'! I atter my 'oman."

Maria placed her hands on the table opposite the man and bent over to look into his face.

"'Oman is all berry much de same," she said in a low, persuasive voice. "Dey comes an' dey goes. One sattify a man quick as annuduh. Dey is lots ob bettuh lookin' gal dan Bess. She fix fuh life now wid dat boy. I ax yuh go an' lef she. Gib she uh chance."

"It tek long time tuh learn one 'oman," he said slowly. "Me an' Bess done fight dat all out dese fibe year gone."

"Yuh ain't goin' leabe she den?" There was an unusual note of pleading in the heavy voice.

"Not till Hell freeze."

After a moment he arose and turned to her.

"I gots tuh go out now. I ain't sho' wedder I goin' away tuhnight or wait fuh tuhmorruh night. I goin' look aroun' an' see how de lan' lay; but I'll be seein' yuh agin befo' I goes."

Maria regarded him for a long moment; the look of sadness in her face deepened to a heavy melancholy; but she said nothing.

Crown started for the street with his long, swaggering stride. The big woman watched him until he turned to the north at the entrance and passed from view. Then she locked the door and, with a deep sigh, walked to her own room.

§

Porgy opened his eyes suddenly. The window, which had been luminous when he went to sleep, was now darkened. He watched it intently. Slowly he realized that parts of the little square still showed the moonlit waters of the bay, and that only the centre was blocked out by an intervening mass. Then the mass moved, and Porgy saw that it was the torso and shoulders of a man. The window was three feet in width, yet the shoulders seemed to brush both sides of it as the form bent forward. The sash was down, and presently there came a sound as though hands were testing it to see whether it could be forced up.

Porgy was lying on his back. He reached his left hand over the covers and let the fingers touch ever so lightly the sleeping faces of first the baby, then the woman. His right hand slid beneath his pillow, and his strong, slender fingers closed about the handle of a knife.

At the window the slight, testing noise continued.

§

It was certainly after midnight when Maria looked from her doorway; for the moon was tottering on the western wall, and while she stood looking, slowly it dropped over and vanished.

The vague forebodings that she had felt when she talked to Crown earlier in the evening had kept sleep from her; with each passing hour her fears increased, and with them a sense of imminence that finally forced her to get up, slip on a wrapper, and prepare to make the rounds of the court.

But on opening her door, she was at once reassured. The square stood before her like a vast cistern brimmed with misty dark and roofed with a lid of sky. A cur grovelled forward on its belly from a near-by nook, and licked one of her bare feet with its moist, warm tongue.

Above her, in the huge honeycomb of the building, someone was snoring in a slow, steady rhythm.

The big negress drew a deep sigh of relief and turned back toward her room.

A sound of cracking wood snapped the silence. Then, like a flurry of small bells, came a shiver of broken glass on the stones.

Maria spun around, and tried to locate the sound; but no noise followed. Silence flowed back over the court and settled pal-

pably into its recesses. The faint, not unpleasant rhythm of the snoring came in-
sistently forward.

Suddenly Maria turned, her face quick
with apprehension. She drew her wrapper
closely about her, and crossed to Porgy's
door. With only half of the distance
traversed, she heard a sound from the room.
It was more of a muffled thump than anything else, and with it, something very like
a gasp.

When her hand closed over the knob all
was silent again, except that she could hear
a long, slightly shuddering breath.

Then came a sound that caused her flesh
to prickle with primal terror. It was so un-
expected, there in the chill, silent night. It
was Porgy's laugh, but different. Out of
the stillness it swelled suddenly, deep,
aboriginal, lustful. Then it stopped
short.

Maria heard the baby cry out; then Bess's
voice, sleepy and mystified. "Fuh Gawd'
sake, Porgy, what yuh laughin' 'bout?"

"Dat all right, honey," came the answer.
"Don't yuh be worryin'. Yuh gots Porgy
now, an' he look atter he 'oman. Ain't I
done tells yuh: Yuh gots er *man* now."

Maria turned the knob, entered the room,
and closed the door quickly behind her.

Night trailed westward across the city.
In the east, out beyond the ocean's rim, es-
sential light trembled upward and seemed
to absorb rather than quench the morning
stars. Out of the sliding planes of mist that
hung like spent breath above the city, shapes
began to emerge and assume their proper
values.

Far in the upper air over Catfish Row a
speck appeared. It took a long, descending
spiral, and became two, then three. Around
a wide circle the specks swung, as though
hung by wires from a lofty pivot. The light
brightened perceptibly. The specks dropped
to a lower level, increased in size, and
miraculously became a dozen. Then some
of them dropped in from the circumference
of the circle, cutting lines across like the
spokes of a wheel, and from time to time
flapping indolent wings. Dark and menacing when they flew to the westward, they
would turn easily toward the east, and the
sun, still below the horizon, would gild their
bodies with ruddy gold, as they sailed,
breast on, toward it.

Down, down they dropped, reaching low,
and yet lower levels, until at last they
seemed to brush the water-front buildings
with their sombre wings. Then gradually
they narrowed to a small circle that pa-

trolled the air directly over a shape that lay
awash in the rising tide, across the street
from Catfish Row.

Suddenly from the swinging circle a single
bird planed down and lit with an awkward,
hopping step directly before the object. For
a moment he regarded it with bleak, preda-
tory eyes; then flew back to his fellows. A
moment later the whole flock swooped down,
and the shape was hidden by flapping wings
and black awkward bodies that hopped
about and fought inward to the centre of
the group.

A negro who had been sleeping under an
overturned bateau awoke and rubbed his
eyes; then he sprang up and, seizing an oar,
beat the birds away with savage blows.

He bent over the object for a moment,
then turned and raced for the street with
eyes showing white.

"Fuh Gawd' sake, folks," he cried, "come
hyuh quick! Hyuh Crown, an' he done
dead."

§

A group of three white men stood over
the body. One was the plain-clothes man
with the goatee and stick who had investi-
gated the Robbins' murder. Behind him

stood a uniformed policeman. The third, a stout, leisurely individual, was stooping over the body, in the act of making an examination.

"What do you make of it, Coroner?" asked the plain-clothes man.

"Knife between fifth and sixth ribs; must have gone straight through the heart."

"Well, he had it comin' to him," the detective observed. "They tell me he is the nigger, Crown, who killed Robbins last April. That gives us the widow to work on fer a starter, by the way; and Hennessy tells me that he used to run with that dope case we had up last August. She's livin' in the Row, too. Let's go over and have a look."

The Coroner cast an apprehensive glance at the forbidding structure across the way.

"Can't be so sure," he cautioned. "Corpse might have been washed up. Tide's on the flood."

"Well, I'm goin' to have a look at those two women, anyway," the plain-clothes man announced. "That place is alive with crooks. I'd like to get something on it that would justify closing it up as a public nuisance, and throwing the whole lot of 'em out in the street. One murder and a happy-dust riot already this summer; and here we are again."

Then turning to the policeman, he gave his orders.

"Get the wagon and take the body in. Then you had better come right back. We might have some arrests. The Coroner and I'll investigate while you're gone."

He turned away toward the Row, assuming that he would be followed.

"All right, Cap; what do you say?" he called.

The Coroner shook his ponderous figure down into his clothes, turned with evident reluctance, and joined him.

"All right," he agreed. "But all I need is a couple of witnesses to identify the body at the inquest."

Across the street a small negro boy detached himself from the base of one of the gateposts and darted through the entrance.

A moment later the white men strode into an absolutely empty square. Their heels made a sharp sound on the flags, and the walls threw a clear echo down upon them.

A cur that had been left napping in the sun woke with a start, looked about in a bewildered fashion, gave a frightened yelp, and bolted through a doorway.

It was all clearly not to the taste of the Coroner, and he cast an uneasy glance about him.

"Where do we go?" he asked.

"That's the widow's room over there, if she hasn't moved. We'll give it a look first," said the detective.

The door was off the latch, and, without knocking, he kicked it open and walked in.

The room was small, but immaculately clean. Beneath a patched white quilt could be seen the form of a woman. Two other women were sitting in utter silence beside the bed.

The form under the covers moaned.

"Drop that," the detective commanded. "And answer some questions."

The moaning stopped.

"Where were you yesterday and last night?"

The reply came slowly, as though speaking were great pain.

"I been sick in dis bed now t'ree day an' night."

"We been settin' wid she, nursin' she, all dat time," one of the women said.

And the other supplemented. "Dat de Gawd' trut'."

"You would swear to that?" asked the Coroner.

Three voices answered in chorus:

"Yes, Boss, we swear tuh dat."

"There you are," said the Coroner to the plain-clothes man, "an air-tight alibi."

The detective regarded him for a moment with supreme contempt. Then he stepped forward and jerked the sheet from Serena's face, which lay upon the pillow as immobile as a model done in brown clay.

"You know damn well that you were out yesterday!" he snapped. "I have a good mind to get the wagon and carry you in."

Silence followed.

"What do you say to that?" he demanded.

But Serena had nothing to say, and neither had her handmaidens.

Then he turned a menacing frown upon them, as they sat motionless with lowered eyes.

"Well!"

They jumped slightly, and their eyes showed white around the iris. Suddenly they began to speak, almost in unison.

"We swear tuh Gawd, we done been hyuh wid she t'ree day."

"Oh, Hell!" said the exasperated detective. "What's the use? You might as well argue with a parrot-cage."

"That woman is just as ill at this moment as you are," he said to his unenthusiastic associate when they were again in the sunlight.

"Her little burlesque show proves that, if nothing else. But there is her case all prepared. I don't believe she killed Crown; she doesn't look like that kind. She is either just playing safe, or she has something entirely different on her chest. But there's her story; and you'll never break in without witnesses of your own; and you'll never get 'em."

The Coroner was not a highly sensitized individual; but as he moved across the empty court, he found it difficult to control his nerves under the scrutiny which he felt leveled upon him from behind a hundred shuttered windows. Twice he caught himself looking covertly over his shoulders; and, as he went, he bore hopefully away toward the entrance.

But the detective was intent upon his task, and presently called him back.

"This is the cripple's room," he said. "He ain't much of a witness. I tried to break him in the Robbins case; but he wouldn't talk. I want to have a look at the woman, though."

He kicked the door open suddenly. Porgy and Bess were seated by the stove, eating breakfast from tin pans. On the bed in the corner the baby lay.

Porgy paused, with his spoon halfway

to his mouth, and looked up. Bess kept her eyes on the pan, and continued to eat.

The Coroner stopped in the doorway, and made a businesslike show of writing in a notebook.

"What's your name?" he asked Porgy.

The cripple studied him for a long moment, taking in the ample proportions of the figure and the heavy, but not unsympathetic, face. Then he smiled one of his fleeting, ingenuous smiles.

"Jus' Porgy," he said. "Yuh knows me, Boss. Yuh is done gib me plenty ob penny on King Charles Street."

"Of course, you're the goat-man. I didn't know you without your wagon," he said amiably. Then, becoming businesslike, he asked:

"This nigger, Crown. You knew him by sight. Didn't you?"

Porgy debated with himself for a moment, looked again into the Coroner's face, was reassured by what he saw there, and replied:

"Yes, Boss; I 'member um w'en he usen tuh come hyuh, long ago."

"You could identify him, I suppose?"

Porgy looked blank.

"You'd know him if you saw him again?"

"Yes, Boss; I know um."

The Coroner made a note in his book, closed it with an air of finality, and put it in his pocket.

During the brief interview, the detective had been making an examination of the room. The floor had been recently scrubbed, and was still damp in the corners. He gave the clean, pine boards a close scrutiny, then paused before the window. The bottom of the lower sash had been broken, and several of the small, square panes were missing.

"So this is where you killed Crown, eh?" he announced.

The words fell into the silence and were absorbed by it, causing them to seem theatrical and unconvincing. Neither Porgy nor Bess spoke. Their faces were blank and noncommittal.

After a full moment, the woman said:

"I ain't onduhstan', Boss. Nobody hyuh ain't kill Crown. My husban' he fall t'rough dat winduh yisterday when he leg gib 'way. He er cripple."

"Any one see him do it?" enquired the Coroner from the door.

"Oh, yes, Boss," replied Bess, turning to him. "T'ree or four ob de mens was in de street; dey will tell yuh all 'bout um."

"Yes, of course; more witnesses," sneered the detective. Then turning to the Coroner, he asked with a trace of sarcasm in his tone:

"That satisfies you fully, I suppose?"

The Coroner's nerves were becoming edgy.

"For God's sake," he retorted, "do you expect me to believe that a cripple could kill a two-hundred pound buck, then tote him a hundred yards? Well, I've got what I need now anyway. As far as I'm concerned, I'm through."

They were passing the door of Maria's shop when the detective caught sight of something within that held his gaze.

"You can do as you please," he told his unwilling companion. "But I'm going to have a look in here. I have never been able to get anything on this woman; but she is a bad influence in the neighborhood. I'd trust her just as far as I could throw her."

The Coroner heaved a sigh of resignation, and they stepped back, and entered the shop.

Upon the flooring, directly before the door, and not far from it, was a pool of blood. Standing over the pool was a table, and upon it lay the carcass of a shark. Maria sat on a bench behind the table. As the men entered she swung an immense cleaver downward. A cross-section of the shark detached itself and fell away on a pile of similar slices. A thin stream of blood dribbled from the table, augmenting the pool upon the floor.

Maria did not raise her eyes from her task. Again the cleaver swung up, and whistled downward.

From the street sounded the clatter of the returning patrol.

"I'll wait for you in the wagon," said the Coroner hastily, and stepped back into the sunlight.

But he was not long alone. The uninterrupted swing of the dripping cleaver was depressing, and the enthusiasm of his associate waned.

The bell clanged. Hoofs struck sparks from the cobbles, and the strong but uncertain arm of the law was withdrawn, to attend to other and more congenial business.

§

The sound from the retreating wagon dwindled and ceased.

For a moment Catfish Row held its breath; then its windows and doors flew open, and poured its life out into the incomparable autumn weather. The crisis had passed. There had been no arrests.

Serena stepped forth, her arms filled with the morning's wash.

" 'Ain't it hahd tuh be er nigger!' " some-one sang in a loud, clear voice. And every-body laughed.

Down the street, like an approaching freight train, came the drays, jarring the building and rattling the windows, as the heavy tires rang against the cobbles.

Bess and Porgy came out with the others, and seated themselves against the wall in the gracious sunlight. Of the life, yet apart from it, sufficient unto each other, they did not join in the loud talk and badinage that was going on about them. Like people who had come on a long, dark journey, they were content to sit, and breathe deeply of the sun. The baby was sleeping in Bess's arms, and from time to time she would sing a stave to it in a soft, husky voice.

Into the court strode a group of steve-dores. Their strong white teeth flashed in the sunshine, and their big, panther-like bod-ies moved easily among the women and chil-dren that crowded about them.

"Wey all de gals?" called one in a loud, resonant voice. "Mus' be dey ain't know dat dis is pay-day."

Two women who were sitting near Porgy and Bess rose and went forward, with their arms twined about each other's waists. In a few minutes they were out of the crowd again, each looking up with admiring eyes into the face of one of the men.

"Mens an' 'omans ain't de same," said Porgy. "One mont' ago dem gals been lib-bin' wid dey own mens. Den de storm tek um. Now dey is fuhgit um a'ready, an' gibbin' dey lub tuh de nex'."

"No; dey is diff'rent fuh true," replied Bess. "An' yuh won't nebber onduhstan'. All two dem gal gots baby fuh keep alibe." She heaved a deep sigh; and then added, "Dey is jus' 'oman, an' nigger at dat. Dey is doin' de bes' dey kin—dat all."

She was looking down at the baby while she spoke, and when she raised her eyes and looked at Porgy, he saw that they were full of tears.

"But you, Bess; you is diff'rent f'om dat?" he said, with a gently interrogating note in his voice.

"Dat 'cause Gawd ain't mek but one Porgy!" she told him. "Any 'oman gots tuh be decent wid you. But I gots fuh tell yuh de trut', widout Porgy I is jus' like de res'."

A shadow drifted across their laps, and they lifted their faces to the sky.

A solitary buzzard had left the circle that had hung high in the air all morning, and was swinging back and forth over the Row, almost brushing the parapet of the roof as

it passed.   While Porgy and Bess looked,
it suddenly raised the points of its wings,
reached tentative legs downward, spread its
feet wide, and lit on the edge of the roof
directly over their room.

"My Gawd!" exclaimed Maria, who was
standing near.   "Crown done sen' he buz-
zud back fuh bring trouble.   Knock um off,
Porgy.   Fer Gawd' sake, knock um off befo'
he settle!"

The cripple reached out and picked up a
brick-bat.   The happiness had left his face,
and his eyes were filled with fear.   With a
swing of his long, powerful arm, he sent the
missile on its errand.

It struck the parapet directly beneath the
bird.

With a spasmodic flap of wings, the black
body lifted itself a few feet from the building, then settled suddenly back.   For a moment it hopped awkwardly about, as though
the roof were red hot beneath its feet, then
folded its wings, drew its nude head in upon
its breast, and surveyed the court with its
aloof, malevolent eyes.

"T'row agin," Maria called, handing
Porgy another brick-bat.   But he seemed not
to hear.   His face quivered, and he hid it in
his hands.

"Sonny," the big negress called to a small boy who was standing near, looking at the bird with his mouth open. "Git out on de roof wid uh stick, an' run dat bird away."

But Porgy plucked at her skirt, and she looked down.

"Let um be," he said in a hopeless voice. "It too late now. Ain't yuh see he done settle, an' he pick my room fuh light ober? It ain't no use now. Yuh knows dat. It ain't no use."

§

The next morning Porgy sat in his accustomed place by Archdale's door. Autumn had touched the oaks in the park across the way, and they brushed the hard, bright sky with a slow circling motion, and tossed handfuls of yellow leaves down upon the pedestrians who stepped briskly along.

King Charles Street was full of hurrying men on their way to the cotton offices and the big wholesale warehouses that fronted on the wharves. Like the artery of a hale old man who has lain long asleep, but who wakens suddenly and springs into a race, the broad thoroughfare seemed to pound and sing with life.

The town was in a generous mood. Again
and again the bottom of Porgy's cup gave
forth its sharp, grateful click as a coin struck
it and settled. But the cripple had not even
his slow glance of thanks for his benefactors
on that flashing autumn morning. Always
he kept veiled, apprehensive eyes directed
either up or down the street, or lifted frightened glances to the sky, as though fearing
what he might see there.

At noon a white man stopped before him.
But he did not drop a coin and pass on.

After a moment, Porgy brought his gaze
back, and looked up.

The white man reached forward, and
handed him a paper.

"Dat fuh me?" asked Porgy, in a voice
that shook.

"You needn't mind takin' it," the man assured him with a laugh. "It's just a sum-
mons as witness to the Coroner's inquest.
You knew that nigger, Crown, didn't you?"

He evidently took Porgy's silence for assent, for he went on.

"Well, all you got to do is to view the
body in the presence of the Coroner, tell him
who it is, and he'll take down all you say."

Porgy essayed speech, failed, tried again,
and finally whispered:

"I gots tuh go an' look on Crown' face

wid all dem w'ite folks lookin' at me. Dat
it?"

His voice was so piteous that the con-
stable reassured him:

"Oh, cheer up; it's not so bad. I reckon
you've seen a dead nigger before this. It
will all be over in a few minutes."

"Dey ain't goin' be no nigger in dat room
'cept me?" Porgy asked.

"Just you and Crown, if you still call him
one."

After a moment Porgy asked:

"I couldn't jus' bring a 'oman wid me?
I couldn't eben carry my—my 'oman?"

"No," said the white man positively.
"Now I've got to be gettin' along, I reckon.
Just come over to the Court House in half
an hour, and I'll meet you and take you in.
Only be sure to come. If you don't show up
it's jail for you, you know."

For a moment after the man had gone,
Porgy sat immovable, with his eyes on the
pavement. Then a sudden change swept
over him. He cast one glance up and down
the hard, clean street, walled by its uncom-
promising, many-eyed buildings. Then in a
panic he clambered into his cart, gave a cruel
twist to the tail of his astonished goat, and
commenced a spasmodic, shambling race up
Meeting House Road in the direction in

which he knew that, miles away, the forests
lay.

§

To many, the scene which ensued on the
upper Meeting House Road stands out as
an exquisitely humorous episode, to be told
and retold with touching up of high lights
and artistic embellishments. To these, in
the eyes of whom the negro is wholly humorous, per se, there was not the omission of a
single conventional and readily recognizable
stage property.

For, after all, what could have been fun-
nier than an entirely serious race between
a negro in a dilapidated goat-cart, and the
municipality's shining new patrol wagon,
fully officered and clanging its bell for the
crowds to hear as it came.

The finish took place in the vicinity of
the railway yards and factories, and the
street was filled with workmen who smoked
against the walls, or ate their lunch, sitting
at the pavement's edge—grand-stand seats,
as they were quite accurately described in the
telling.

The street cars ran seldom that far out;
and Porgy had the thoroughfare almost entirely to himself. His face wore a demented
look, and was working pitifully. In his

panic, he wrung the tail of his unfortunate beast without mercy. The lunchers along the pavement saw him coming, and called to friends further along; so that as he came, he was greeted with shouts of laughter and witty sallies from the crowd.

Then the wagon appeared, a mere speck in the distance, but sending the sound of its bell before it as an advertisement of its presence. It grew rapidly until it reached the cheering crowds. Then it seemed that even the sedate officers of the law were not above a sly humor of their own, for the vehicle slackened its pace perceptibly and prolonged the final moment of capture.

The big buildings had been left behind, and there lay before Porgy only the scattered, cheap bungalows of the labor quarters; and beyond, as elusive and desirable as the white man's heaven, glimmered the far line of the woods, misty and beautiful in the pink autumn haze.

The patrol forged ahead and came to a clanging stop. The officers leapt out and, amid shouts of laughter from the crowd, lifted wagon, goat and man into the vehicle. The driver jerked the horse back into its breechings, swung the wagon with a dramatic snap that was not wasted upon his gallery, and sent it clanging and rocking back in the direction from which it had come.

Porgy fell forward, with his arms thrown out upon the back of the goat, and buried his face between them in the shaggy, evil-smelling hair.

The workmen upon the sidewalks cheered and shouted with mirth. Surely it had been a great day. They would not soon have another laugh to match it.

§

When the wagon reached the down-town district, the inquest was over. It had been a simple matter to secure another witness for the identification of the body. The jury had made short work of their task, and had found that Crown had come to his death as the result of a chest wound at the hands of person or persons unknown.

Porgy was taken at once to the station house, where the charge of "Contempt of Court" was formally entered against him on the blotter, and he was locked up to await trial early the following morning.

Under the wheezing gas jet, the Recorder looked Porgy over with his weary glance, brought the tips of his slender fingers together; gave him "five days," in his tired drawl, and raised his eyes to the next negro on the morning's list.

They hoisted the outfit, goat and all, into the patrol for the trip to the jail, thus again brightening a day for a group of light-hearted Nordics upon the pavement.

A large, red-faced policeman took his seat at the rear of the wagon.

"You sure beat all!" he confided to Porgy, with a puzzled frown. "Runnin' away like the devil was after you, from bein' a witness; an' now goin' to jail with a face like Sunday mornin'."

§

In the fresh beauty of an early October morning, Porgy returned home. There were few of his friends about, as work was now plentiful, and most of those who could earn a day's wage were up and out. He drove through the entrance, pulled his goat up short, and looked about him.

Serena was seated on her bench with a baby in her arms.

Porgy gave her a long look, and a question commenced to dawn in his eyes. The child turned in her arms, and his suspicions were confirmed. It was his baby—his and Bess's.

Then Serena looked up and saw him. She arose in great confusion, clasped the infant to her ample bosom, and, without a word of greeting, stepped through her doorway. Then, as though struck by an afterthought, she turned, thrust her head back through the opening, and called loudly:

"Oh, Maria! hyuh Porgy come home."

Then she disappeared and the door slammed shut.

Mystified and filled with alarm, Porgy turned his vehicle toward the cook-shop and arrived at the door just as Maria stepped over the threshold.

She seated herself on the sill and brought her face level with his. Then she looked into his eyes.

What Porgy saw there caused him to call out sharply:

"Where's Bess? Tell me, quick, where's Bess?"

The big negress did not answer, and after a moment her ponderous face commenced to shake.

Porgy beat the side of his wagon with his fist.

"Where, where—" he began, in a voice that was suddenly shrill.

But Maria placed a steadying hand over his frantic one and held it still.

"Dem dutty dogs got she one day w'en I gone out," she said in a low, shaken voice. "She been missin' yuh an' berry low in she min' 'cause she can't fin' out how long yuh is lock up fuh. Dat damn houn' she knock off de wharf las' summer fin' she like dat an' git she tuh tek er swalluh ob licker. Den half a dozen of de mens gang she, an' mek she drunk."

"But wuh she now?" Porgy cried. "I ain't keer ef she wuz drunk. I want she now."

Maria tried to speak, but her voice refused to do her bidding. She covered her face with her hands, and her throat worked convulsively.

Porgy clutched her wrist. "Tell me," he commanded. "Tell me, now."

"De mens all carry she away on de ribber boat," she sobbed. "Dey leabe word fuh me dat dey goin' tek she all de way tuh Sawannah, an' keep she dey. Den Serena, she tek de chile, an' say she is goin' gib um er Christian raisin'."

Deep sobs stopped Maria's voice. For a while she sat there, her face buried in her hands. But Porgy had nothing to say. When she finally raised her head and looked at him, she was surprised at what she saw.

The keen autumn sun flooded boldly

through the entrance and bathed the drooping form of the goat, the ridiculous wagon,
and the bent figure of the man in hard,
satirical radiance. In its revealing light,
Maria saw that Porgy was an old man. The
early tension that had characterized him, the
mellow mood that he had known for one
eventful summer, both had gone; and in
their place she saw a face that sagged wearily, and the eyes of age lit only by a faint
reminiscent glow from suns and moons that
had looked into them, and had already
dropped down the west.

She looked until she could bear the sight
no longer; then she stumbled into her shop
and closed the door, leaving Porgy and the
goat alone in an irony of morning sunlight.

THE END